Henry James

The private life of Lord Beaupré

The visits

Henry James

The private life of Lord Beaupré
The visits

ISBN/EAN: 9783744749312

Printed in Europe, USA, Canada, Australia, Japan

Cover: Foto ©Raphael Reischuk / pixelio.de

More available books at **www.hansebooks.com**

The Private Life
Lord Beaupré
The Visits

BY

HENRY JAMES

NEW YORK
HARPER & BROTHERS PUBLISHERS
1893

CONTENTS

THE PRIVATE LIFE

THE PRIVATE LIFE

WE talked of London, face to face with a great bristling, primeval glacier. The hour and the scene were one of those impressions which make up a little, in Switzerland, for the modern indignity of travel— the promiscuities and vulgarities, the station and the hotel, the gregarious patience, the struggle for a scrappy attention, the reduction to a numbered state. The high valley was pink with the mountain rose, the cool air as fresh as if the world were young. There was a faint flush of afternoon on undiminished snows, and the fraternizing tinkle of the unseen cattle came to us with a cropped and sun-warmed odor. The balconied inn stood on the very neck of the sweetest pass in the Oberland, and for a week we had had company and weather. This was felt to be great luck, for one would have made up for the other had either been bad.

The weather certainly would have made up for the company; but it was not subjected to this tax, for we had by a happy chance the *fleur des pois :* Lord and Lady Mellifont, Clare Vawdrey, the greatest (in the opinion of many) of our literary glories, and Blanche Adney, the greatest (in the opinion of all) of our theatrical. I mention these first, because they were just the people whom in London, at that time, people tried to "get." People endeavored to "book" them six weeks ahead, yet on this occasion we had come in for them, we had all come in for each other, without the least wire-pulling. A turn of the game had pitched us together, the last of August, and we recognized our luck by remaining so, under protection of the barometer. When the golden days were over—that would come soon enough—we should wind down opposite sides of the pass and disappear over the crest of surrounding heights. We were of the same general communion, we participated in the same miscellaneous publicity. We met, in London, with irregular frequency; we were more or less governed by the laws and the language, the traditions and the shibboleths of the same dense social state. I think all of us, even the ladies, "did" something, though we pretended we didn't when it was mentioned. Such things are not mentioned indeed in London, but it was our innocent pleasure to be different here. There had to be some way to show the difference, inasmuch as we were under the impression that this was our annual holiday. We felt at any rate that the conditions were more human than in London, or that at least we ourselves were. We were frank about this, we talked about it : it was what we were talking about as we looked at the flushing glacier, just as some one called attention to the prolonged absence of Lord Mellifont and Mrs. Adney. We were seated on the terrace of the inn, where there were benches and little tables, and those of us who were most bent on proving that we had returned to nature were, in the queer Germanic fashion, having coffee before meat.

The remark about the absence of our
two companions was not taken up, not even
by Lady Mellifont, not even by little Adney, the fond composer, for it had been
dropped only in the briefest intermission of
Clare Vawdrey's talk. (This celebrity was
"Clarence" only on the title-page.) It
was just that revelation of our being after
all human that was his theme. He asked
the company whether, candidly, every one
hadn't been tempted to say to every one
else, "I had no idea you were really so
nice." I had had, for my part, an idea that
he was, and even a good deal nicer, but that
was too complicated to go into then, besides it is exactly my story. There was a
general understanding among us that when
Vawdrey talked we should be silent, and
not, oddly enough, because he at all expected it. He didn't, for of all abundant
talkers he was the most unconscious, the
least greedy and professional. It was rather
the religion of the host, of the hostess, that
prevailed among us; it was their own idea,
but they always looked for a listening circle
when the great novelist dined with them.

On the occasion I allude to there was probably no one present with whom, in London, he had not dined, and we felt the force of this habit. He had dined even with me ; and on the evening of that dinner, as on this Alpine afternoon, I had been at no pains to hold my tongue, absorbed as I inveterately was in a study of the question which always rose before me, to such a height, in his fair, square, strong stature.

This question was all the more tormenting that he never suspected himself (I am sure) of imposing it, any more than he had ever observed that every day of his life every one listened to him at dinner. He used to be called "subjective" in the weekly papers, but in society no distinguished man could have been less so. He never talked about himself; and this was a topic on which, though it would have been tremendously worthy of him, he apparently never even reflected. He had his hours and his habits, his tailor and his hatter, his hygiene and his particular wine, but all these things together never made up an attitude. Yet they constituted the only attitude he ever adopted, and it was easy for him to refer to our being " nicer " abroad than at home. *He* was exempt from variations, and not a shade either less or more nice in one place than in another. He differed from other people, but never from himself (save in the extraordinary sense which I will presently explain), and struck me as having neither moods nor sensibilities nor preferences. He might have been always in the same company, so far as he recognized any influence from age or condition or sex: he addressed himself to women exactly as he addressed himself to men, and gossiped with all men alike, talking no better to clever folk than to dull. I used to feel a despair at his way of liking one subject—so far as I could tell—precisely as much as another: there were some I hated so myself. I never found him anything but loud and cheerful and copious, and I never heard him utter a paradox or express a shade or play with an idea. That fancy about our being " human " was, in his conversation, quite an exceptional flight.

His opinions were sound and second-rate, and of his perceptions it was too mystifying to think. I envied him his magnificent health.

Vawdrey had marched, with his even pace and his perfectly good conscience, into the flat country of anecdote, where stories are visible from afar like windmills and signposts ; but I observed after a little that Lady Mellifont's attention wandered. I happened to be sitting next her. I noticed that her eyes rambled a little anxiously over the lower slopes of the mountains. At last, after looking at her watch, she said to me : "Do you know where they went ?"

"Do you mean Mrs. Adney and Lord Mellifont ?"

"Lord Mellifont and Mrs. Adney." Her ladyship's speech seemed—unconsciously indeed—to correct me, but it didn't occur to me that this was because she was jealous. I imputed to her no such vulgar sentiment ; in the first place because I liked her, and in the second because it would always occur to one quickly that it was right, in

any connection, to put Lord Mellifont first.
He *was* first — extraordinarily first. I
don't say greatest or wisest or most re-
nowned, but essentially at the top of the
list and the head of the table. That is a
position by itself, and his wife was naturally
accustomed to see him in it. My phrase
had sounded as if Mrs. Adney had taken
him ; but it was not possible for him to be
taken—he only took. No one, in the nature
of things, could know this better than Lady
Mellifont. I had originally been rather
afraid of her, thinking her, with her stiff
silences and the extreme blackness of almost everything that made up her person,
somewhat hard, even a little saturnine.
Her paleness seemed slightly gray, and her
glossy black hair metallic, like the brooches
and bands and combs with which it was
inveterately adorned. She was in perpetual
mourning, and wore numberless ornaments
of jet and onyx, a thousand clicking chains
and bugles and beads. I had heard Mrs.
Adney call her the queen of night, and the
term was descriptive if you understood that
the night was cloudy. She had a secret,

and if you didn't find it out as you knew her better, you at least perceived that she was gentle and unaffected and limited, and also rather submissively sad. She was like a woman with a painless malady. I told her that I had merely seen her husband and his companion stroll down the glen together about an hour before, and suggested that Mr. Adney would perhaps know something of their intentions.

Vincent Adney, who, though he was fifty years old, looked like a good little boy on whom it had been impressed that children should not talk before company, acquitted himself with remarkable simplicity and taste of the position of husband of a great exponent of comedy. When all was said about her making it easy for him, one couldn't help admiring the charmed affection with which he took everything for granted. It is difficult for a husband who is not on the stage, or at least in the theatre, to be graceful about a wife who is; but Adney was more than graceful—he was exquisite, he was inspired. He set his beloved to music; and you remember how genuine his music

could be—the only English compositions I
ever saw a foreigner take an interest in.
His wife was in them, somewhere, always;
they were like a free, rich translation of the
impression she produced. She seemed, as
one listened, to pass laughing, with loosened
hair across the scene. He had been only
a little fiddler at her theatre, always in his
place during the acts; but she had made
him something rare and misunderstood.
Their superiority had become a kind of
partnership, and their happiness was a part
of the happiness of their friends. Adney's
one discomfort was that he couldn't write a
play for his wife, and the only way he med-
dled with her affairs was by asking impossible people if *they* couldn't.

Lady Mellifont, after looking across at
him a moment, remarked to me that she
would rather not put any question to
him. She added the next minute: " I
had rather people shouldn't see I'm nervous."

" *Are* you nervous ? "

" I always become so if my husband is
away from me for any time."

"Do you imagine something has happened to him?"

"Yes, always. Of course I'm used to it."

"Do you mean his tumbling over precipices—that sort of thing?"

"I don't know exactly what it is; it's the general sense that he'll never come back."

She said so much and kept back so much that the only way to treat the condition she referred to seemed the jocular. "Surely he'll never forsake you!" I laughed.

She looked at the ground a moment. "Oh, at bottom I'm easy."

"Nothing can ever happen to a man so accomplished, so infallible, so armed at all points," I went on, encouragingly.

"Oh, you don't know how he's armed!" she exclaimed, with such an odd quaver that I could account for it only by her being nervous. This idea was confirmed by her moving just afterwards, changing her seat rather pointlessly, not as if to cut our conversation short, but because she was in a fidget. I couldn't know what was the matter with her, but I was presently relieved to see Mrs. Adney come towards us. She had in her hand a big bunch of wild flowers, but she was not closely attended by Lord Mellifont. I quickly saw, however, that she had no disaster to announce; yet, as I knew there was a question Lady Mellifont would like to hear answered, but did not wish to ask, I expressed to her immediately the hope that his lordship had not remained in a crevasse.

"Oh, no; he left me but three minutes ago. He has gone into the house." Blanche Adney rested her eyes on mine an instant— a mode of intercourse to which no man, for himself, could ever object. The interest, on this occasion, was quickened by the particular thing the eyes happened to say. What they usually said was only, "Oh, yes, I'm charming, I know, but don't make a fuss about it. I only want a new part—I do, I do!" At present they added, dimly, surreptitiously, and of course sweetly—for that was the way they did everything: "It's all right; but something did happen. Perhaps I'll tell you later." She turned to Lady Mellifont, and the transition to simple gayety suggested her mastery of her profession. "I've brought him safe; we had a charming walk."

"I'm so very glad," returned Lady Mellifont, with her faint smile, continuing vaguely, as she got up, "he must have gone to dress for dinner. Isn't it rather near?" She moved away, to the hotel, in her leave-taking, simplifying fashion, and the rest of us, at the mention of dinner, looked at each other's watches, as if to shift the responsibility of such grossness. The head-waiter, essentially, like all head-waiters, a man of the world, allowed us hours and places of our own, so that in the evening, apart under the lamp, we formed a compact, an indulged little circle. But it was only the Mellifonts who "dressed" and as to whom it was recognized that they naturally *would* dress : she in exactly the same manner as on any other evening of her ceremonious existence (she was not a woman whose habits could take account of anything so mutable as fitness); and he, on the other hand, with remarkable adjustment and suitability. He was almost as much a man of the world as the head-waiter, and spoke almost as many languages;

but he abstained from courting a comparison of dress-coats and white waistcoats, analyzing the occasion in a much finer way—into black velvet and blue velvet and brown velvet, for instance, into delicate harmonies of necktie and subtle informalities of shirt. He had a costume for every function and a moral for every costume ; and his functions and costumes and morals were ever a part of the amusement of life—a part at any rate of its beauty and romance—for an immense circle of spectators. For his particular friends indeed these things were more than an amusement; they were a topic, a social support, and of course, in addition, a subject of perpetual suspense. If his wife had not been present before dinner they were what the rest of us probably would have been putting our heads together about.

Clare Vawdrey had a fund of anecdote on the whole question : he had known Lord Mellifont almost from the beginning. It was a peculiarity of this nobleman that there could be no conversation about him that didn't instantly take the form of anecdote, and a still further distinction that

there could apparently be no anecdote that
was not on the whole to his honor. If he
had come into a room at any moment, people might have said frankly, " Of course we
were telling stories about you !" As con-
sciences go, in London, the general conscience would have been good. Moreover,
it would have been impossible to imagine
his taking such a tribute otherwise than
amiably, for he was always as unperturbed
as an actor with the right cue. He had
never in his life needed the prompter—his
very embarrassments had been rehearsed.
For myself, when he was talked about I always had an odd impression that we were
speaking of the dead—it was with that pe-
culiar accumulation of relish. His reputation was a kind of gilded obelisk, as if he
had been buried beneath it; the body of
legend and reminiscence, of which he was
to be the subject, had crystallized in advance.

This ambiguity sprang, I suppose, from
the fact that the mere sound of his name
and air of his person, the general expecta-
tion he created, were, somehow, too exalted

to be verified. The experience of his ur-
banity always came later; the prefigure-
ment, the legend paled before the reality.
I remember that on the evening I refer to
the reality was particularly operative. The
handsomest man of his period could never
have looked better, and he sat among us
like a bland conductor controlling by an
harmonious play of arm an orchestra still a
little rough. He directed the conversation
by gestures as irresistible as they were
vague; one felt as if without him it wouldn't
have had anything to call a tone. This was
essentially what he contributed to any occasion — what he contributed above all to
English public life. He pervaded it, he
colored it, he embellished it, and without
him it would scarcely have had a vocabu-
lary; certainly it would not have had a
style, for a style was what it had in having
Lord Mellifont. He *was* a style. I was
freshly struck with it as, in the *salle à man-
ger* of the little Swiss inn, we resigned ourselves to inevitable veal. Confronted with
his form (I must parenthesize that it was
not confronted much), Clare Vawdrey's talk

suggested the reporter contrasted with the bard. It was interesting to watch the shock of characters from which, of an evening, so much would be expected. There was, however, no concussion—it was all muffled and minimized in Lord Mellifont's tact. It was rudimentary with him to find the solution of such a problem in playing the host, assuming responsibilities which carried with them their sacrifice. He had, indeed, never been a guest in his life; he was the host, the patron, the moderator at every board. If there was a defect in his manner (and I suggest it under my breath), it was that he had a little more art than any conjunction— even the most complicated—could possibly require. At any rate, one made one's reflections in noticing how the accomplished peer handled the situation, and how the sturdy man of letters was unconscious that the situation (and least of all he himself as part of it) was handled. Lord Mellifont poured forth treasures of tact, and Clare Vawdrey never dreamed he was doing it.

Vawdrey had no suspicion of any such precaution, even when Blanche Adney asked

him if he saw yet their third act—an inquiry into which she introduced a subtlety of
her own. She had a theory that he was to
write her a play, and that the heroine, if he
would only do his duty, would be the part
for which she had immemorially longed.
She was forty years old (this could be no
secret to those who had admired her from
the first), and she could now reach out her
hand and touch her uttermost goal. This
gave a kind of tragic passion—perfect actress
of comedy as she was—to her desire not to
miss the great thing. The years had passed,
and still she had missed it; none of the
things she had done was the thing she had
dreamed of, so that at present there was no
more time to lose. This was the canker in
the rose, the ache beneath the smile. It
made her touching—made her sadness even
sweeter than her laughter. She had done
the old English and the new French, and
had charmed her generation; but she was
haunted by the vision of a bigger chance,
of something truer to the conditions that
lay near her. She was tired of Sheridan
and she hated Bowdler; she called for a

canvas of a finer grain. The worst of it, to my sense, was that she would never extract her modern comedy from the great mature novelist, who was as incapable of producing it as he was of threading a needle. She coddled him, she talked to him, she made love to him, as she frankly proclaimed; but she dwelt in illusions—she would have to live and die with Bowdler.

It is difficult to be cursory over this charming woman, who was beautiful without beauty and complete with a dozen deficiencies. The perspective of the stage made her over, and in society she was like the model off the pedestal. She was the picture walking about, which to the artless social mind was a perpetual surprise—a miracle. People thought she told them the secrets of the pictorial nature, in return for which they gave her relaxation and tea. She told them nothing and she drank the tea; but they had, all the same, the best of the bargain. Vawdrey was really at work on a play; but if he had begun it because he liked her, I think he let it drag for the same reason. He secretly felt the atrocious difficulty—

knew that from his hand the finished piece
would have received no active life. At the
same time, nothing could be more agreeable
than to have such a question open with
Blanche Adney, and from time to time he
put something very good into the play. If
he deceived Mrs. Adney, it was only because
in her despair she was determined to be deceived. To her question about their third
act he replied that before dinner he had
written a magnificent passage.

"Before dinner?" I said. "Why, *cher
maître*, before dinner you were holding us
all spellbound on the terrace."

My words were a joke, because I thought
his had been; but for the first time that I
could remember I perceived a certain confusion in his face. He looked at me hard,
throwing back his head quickly, the least bit
like a horse who has been pulled up short.
"Oh, it was before that," he replied, naturally enough.

"Before that you were playing billiards
with *me*," Lord Mellifont intimated.

"Then it must have been yesterday,"
said Vawdrey.

But he was in a tight place. "You told me this morning you did nothing yesterday," the actress objected.

"I don't think I really know when I do things." Vawdrey looked vaguely, without helping himself, at a dish that was offered him.

"It's enough if *we* know," smiled Lord Mellifont.

"I don't believe you've written a line," said Blanche Adney.

"I think I could repeat you the scene." Vawdrey helped himself to *haricots verts*.

"Oh, do! oh, do!" two or three of us cried.

"After dinner, in the salon; it will be an immense *régal*," Lord Mellifont declared.

"I'm not sure, but I'll try," Vawdrey went on.

"Oh, you lovely man!" exclaimed the actress, who was practising Americanisms, being resigned even to an American comedy.

"But there must be this condition," said Vawdrey: "you must make your husband play."

" Play while you're reading ?   Never !"

" I've too much vanity," said Adney.

Lord Mellifont distinguished him.   "You must give us the overture before the curtain rises.   That's a peculiarly delightful moment."

" I sha'n't read—I shall just speak," said Vawdrey.

" Better still; let me go and get your manuscript," the actress suggested.

Vawdrey replied that the manuscript didn't matter; but an hour later, in the salon, we wished he might have had it. We sat expectant, still under the spell of Adney's violin.   His wife, in the foreground on an ottoman, was all impatience and profile, and Lord Mellifont, in the chair — it was always *the* chair, Lord Mellifont's— made our grateful little group feel like a social science congress or a distribution of prizes. Suddenly, instead of beginning, our tame lion began to roar out of tune—he had clean forgotten every word.   He was very sorry, but the lines absolutely wouldn't come to him; he was utterly ashamed, but his memory was a blank.   He didn't look in

the least ashamed — Vawdrey had never
looked ashamed in his life; he was only
imperturbably and merrily natural. He
protested that he had never expected to
make such a fool of himself, but we felt
that this wouldn't prevent the incident from
taking its place among his jolliest reminiscences. It was only *we* who were humili-
ated, as if he had played us a premeditated
trick. This was an occasion, if ever, for
Lord Mellifont's tact, which descended on
us all like balm. He told us, in his charming, artistic way, his way of bridging over
arid intervals (he had a *débit*—there was
nothing to approach it in England — like
the actors of the Comédie Française), of his
own collapse on a momentous occasion, the
delivery of an address to a mighty multi-
tude, when, finding he had forgotten his
memoranda, he fumbled on the terrible platform, the cynosure of every eye, fumbled
vainly in irreproachable pockets for indis-
pensable notes. But the point of his story
was finer than that of Vawdrey's pleasantry;
for he sketched with a few light gestures the
brilliancy of a performance which had risen

superior to embarrassment — had resolved
itself, we were left to divine, into an effort
recognized at the moment as not absolutely
a blot on what the public was so good as to
call his reputation.

"Play up—play up!" cried Blanche Adney, tapping her husband, and remembering
how, on the stage, a *contretemps* is always
drowned in music. Adney threw himself
upon his fiddle, and I said to Clare Vawdrey that his mistake could easily be cor-
rected by his sending for the manuscript.
If he would tell me where it was I would immediately fetch it from his room. To this
he replied, "My dear fellow, I'm afraid there
is no manuscript."

"Then you've not written anything?"

"I'll write it to-morrow."

"Ah, you trifle with us!" I said, in much
mystification.

Vawdrey hesitated an instant. "If there
is anything, you'll find it on my table."

At this moment one of the others spoke
to him, and Lady Mellifont remarked audi-
bly, as if to correct gently our want of consideration, that Mr. Adney was playing some-

thing very beautiful. I had noticed before that she appeared extremely fond of music; she always listened to it in a hushed transport. Vawdrey's attention was drawn away, but it didn't seem to me that the words he had just dropped constituted a definite permission to go to his room. Moreover, I wanted to speak to Blanche Adney; I had something to ask her. I had to await my chance, however, as we remained silent awhile for her husband, after which the conversation became general. It was our habit to go to bed early, but there was still a little of the evening left. Before it quite waned I found an opportunity to tell the actress that Vawdrey had given me leave to put my hand on his manuscript. She adjured me, by all I held sacred, to bring it immediately, to give it to her; and her insistence was proof against my suggestion that it would now be too late for him to begin to read; besides which, the charm was broken—the others wouldn't care. It was not too late for *her* to begin; therefore I was to possess myself, without more delay, of the precious pages. I told her she should be obeyed in a moment, but I wanted her first to satisfy my just curiosity. What had happened before dinner, while she was on the hills with Lord Mellifont?

"How do you know anything happened?"

"I saw it in your face when you came back."

"And they call me an actress!" cried Mrs. Adney.

"What do they call *me* ?" I inquired.

"You're a searcher of hearts—that frivolous thing, an observer."

"I wish you'd let an observer write you a play!" I broke out.

"People don't care for what you write; you'd break any run of luck."

"Well, I see plays all around me," I declared; "the air is full of them to-night."

"The air? Thank you for nothing! I only wish my table-drawers were."

"Did he make love to you on the glacier?" I went on.

She stared; then broke into the graduated ecstasy of her laugh. "Lord Mellifont, poor dear? What a funny place! It would indeed be the place for *our* love !"

"Did he fall into a crevasse?" I continued.

Blanche Adney looked at me again as she had done for an instant when she came up, before dinner, with her hands full of flowers. "I don't know into what he fell. I'll tell you to-morrow."

"He did come down, then?"

"Perhaps he went up," she laughed. "It's really strange!"

"All the more reason you should tell me to-night."

"I must think it over; I must puzzle it out."

"Oh, if you want conundrums, I'll throw in another," I said. "What's the matter with the master?"

"The master of what?"

"Of every form of dissimulation. Vawdrey hasn't written a line."

"Go and get his papers, and we'll see."

"I don't like to expose him," I said.

"Why not, if I expose Lord Mellifont?"

"Oh, I'd do anything for that," I conceded. "But why should Vawdrey have made a false statement? It's very curious."

" It's very curious," Blanche Adney repeated, with a musing air and her eyes on
Lord Mellifont. Then, rousing herself, she
added : " Go and look in his room."

" In Lord Mellifont's ?"

She turned to me quickly. "*That* would
be a way !"

" A way to what ?"

" To find out—to find out !" She spoke
gayly and excitedly, but suddenly checked
herself. " We're talking nonsense," she
said.

" We're mixing things up, but I'm struck
with your idea. Get Lady Mellifont to let
you."

" Oh, *she* has looked !" Mrs. Adney murmured, with the oddest dramatic expression.
Then, after a movement of her beautiful uplifted hand, as if to brush away a fantastic
vision, she exclaimed, imperiously : " Bring
me the scene—bring me the scene !"

" I go for it," I answered; " but don't tell
me I can't write a play."

She left me, but my errand was arrested
by the approach of a lady who had produced
a birthday-book—we had been threatened

with it for several evenings—and who did me the honor to solicit my autograph. She had been asking the others, and she couldn't decently leave me out. I could usually remember my name, but it always took me some time to recall my date, and even when I had done so I was never very sure. I hesitated between two days, and I remarked to my petitioner that I would sign on both if it would give her any satisfaction. She said that surely I had been born only once; and I replied of course that on the day I made her acquaintance I had been born again. I mention the feeble joke only to show that, with the obligatory inspection of the other autographs, we gave some minutes to this transaction. The lady departed with her book, and then I became aware that the company had dispersed. I was alone in the little salon that had been appropriated to our use. My first impression was one of disappointment: if Vawdrey had gone to bed I didn't wish to disturb him. While I hesitated, however, I recognized that Vawdrey had not gone to bed. A window was open, and the sound of voices outside came in to me; Blanche was on the terrace with her dramatist, and they were talking about the stars. I went to the window for a glimpse — the Alpine night was splendid. My friends had stepped out together; the actress had picked up a cloak; she looked as I had seen her look in the wing of the theatre. They were silent awhile, and I heard the roar of a neighboring torrent. I turned back into the room, and its quiet lamplight gave me an idea. Our companions had dispersed—it was late for a pastoral country—and we three should have the place to ourselves. Clare Vawdrey had written his scene—it was magnificent; and his reading it to us there, at such an hour, would be an episode intensely memorable. I would bring down his manuscript and meet the two with it as they came in.

I quitted the salon for this purpose; I had been in Vawdrey's room and knew it was on the second floor, the last in a long corridor. A minute later my hand was on the knob of his door, which I naturally pushed open without knocking. It was equally natural that in the absence of its

occupant the room should be dark; the
more so as, the end of the corridor being at
that hour unlighted, the obscurity was not
immediately diminished by the opening of
the door. I was only aware at first that I
had made no mistake and that, the window-
curtains not being drawn, I was confronted
with a couple of vague, starlighted apertures.
Their aid, however, was not sufficient to en-
able me to find what I had come for, and
my hand, in my pocket, was already on the
little box of matches that I always carried
for cigarettes. Suddenly I withdrew it with
a start, uttering an ejaculation, an apology.
I had entered the wrong room; a glance
prolonged for three seconds showed me a
figure seated at a table near one of the
windows—a figure I had at first taken for a
travelling-rug thrown over a chair. I re-
treated, with a sense of intrusion; but as I
did so I became aware, more rapidly than it
takes me to express it, in the first place
that this was Vawdrey's room, and in the
second that, most singularly, Vawdrey himself sat before me. Checking myself on the
threshold I had a momentary feeling of be-

3

wilderment, but before I knew it I had exclaimed: "Hullo! is that you, Vawdrey?"

He neither turned nor answered me, but my question received an immediate and practical reply in the opening of a door on the other side of the passage. A servant, with a candle, had come out of the opposite room, and in this flitting illumination I definitely recognized the man whom, an instant before, I had to the best of my belief left below in conversation with Mrs. Adney. His back was half turned to me, and he bent over the table in the attitude of writing, but I was conscious that I was in no sort of error about his identity. "I beg your pardon; I thought you were downstairs," I said; and as the personage gave no sign of hearing me I added, "If you're busy I won't disturb you." I backed out, closing the door—I had been in the place, I suppose, less than a minute. I had a sense of mystification, which however deepened infinitely the next instant. I stood there with my hand still on the knob of the door, overtaken by the oddest impression of my life. Vawdrey was at his table, writing,

and it was a very natural place for him to
be ; but why was he writing in the dark, and
why hadn't he answered me ? I waited a
few seconds for the sound of some movement, to see if he wouldn't rouse himself
from his abstraction—a fit conceivable in a
great writer—and call out : " Oh, my dear
fellow, is it you ?" But I heard only the
stillness, I felt only the starlighted dusk of
the room, with the unexpected presence it
enclosed. I turned away, slowly retracing
my steps, and came confusedly down-stairs.
The lamp was still burning in the salon, but
the room was empty. I passed round to
the door of the hotel and stepped out.
Empty too was the terrace. Blanche Adney
and the gentleman with her had apparently
come in. I hung about five minutes ; then
I went to bed.

I slept badly, for I was agitated. On
looking back at these queer occurrences
(you will see presently that they were queer),
I perhaps suppose myself more agitated
than I was ; for great anomalies are never
so great at first as after we have reflected
upon them. It takes us some time to ex-

haust explanations. I was vaguely nervous
—I had been sharply startled; but there was
nothing I could not clear up by asking
Blanche Adney, the first thing in the morning,
who had been with her on the terrace. Oddly
enough, however, when the morning dawned
—it dawned admirably—I felt less desire to
satisfy myself on this point than to escape,
to brush away the shadow of my stupefaction. I saw the day would be splendid, and
the fancy took me to spend it, as I had
spent happy days of youth, in a lonely
mountain ramble. I dressed early, partook
of conventional coffee, put a big roll into
one pocket and a small flask into the other,
and, with a stout stick in my hand, went forth
into the high places. My story is not closely
concerned with the charming hours I passed
there—hours of the kind that make intense
memories. If I roamed away half of them
on the shoulders of the hills, I lay on the
sloping grass for the other half and, with
my cap pulled over my eyes (save a peep
for immensities of view), listened, in the
bright stillness, to the mountain bee and
felt most things sink and dwindle. Clare

Vawdrey grew small, Blanche Adney grew dim, Lord Mellifont grew old, and before the day was over I forgot that I had ever been puzzled. When in the late afternoon I made my way down to the inn there was nothing I wanted so much to find out as whether dinner would not soon be ready. To-night I dressed, in a manner, and by the time I was presentable they were all at table.

In their company again my little problem came back to me, so that I was curious to see if Vawdrey wouldn't look at me the least bit queerly. But he didn't look at me at all; which gave me a chance both to be patient and to wonder why I should hesitate to ask him my question across the table. I did hesitate, and with the consciousness of doing so came back a little of the agitation I had left behind me, or below me, during the day. I wasn't ashamed of my scruple, however: it was only a fine discretion. What I vaguely felt was that a public inquiry wouldn't have been fair. Lord Mellifont was there, of course, to mitigate with his perfect manner all consequences; but I think it was present to me that with these particular elements his lordship would not be at home. The moment we got up, therefore, I approached Mrs. Adney, asking her whether, as the evening was lovely, she wouldn't take a turn with me outside.

"You've walked a hundred miles; had you not better be quiet?" she replied.

"I'd walk a hundred miles more to get you to tell me something."

She looked at me an instant, with a little of the queerness I had sought, but had not found, in Clare Vawdrey's eyes. "Do you mean what became of Lord Mellifont?"

"Of Lord Mellifont?" With my new speculation I had lost that thread.

"Where's your memory, foolish man? We talked of it last evening."

"Ah, yes!" I cried, recalling; "we shall have lots to discuss." I drew her out to the terrace, and before we had gone three steps I said to her: "Who was with you here last night?"

"Last night?" she repeated, as wide of the mark as I had been.

"At ten o'clock—just after our company

broke up. You came out here with a gentleman; you talked about the stars."

She stared a moment; then she gave her
laugh. "Are you jealous of dear Vawdrey?"

"Then it was he?"

"Certainly it was."

"And how long did he stay?"

"You have it badly. He stayed about a
quarter of an hour — perhaps rather more.
We walked some distance; he talked about
his play. There you have it all; that is the
only witchcraft I have used."

"And what did Vawdrey do afterwards?"

"I haven't the least idea. I left him and
went to bed."

"At what time did you go to bed?"

"At what time did *you?* I happen to remember that I parted from Mr. Vawdrey at
ten twenty-five," said Mrs. Adney. "I came
back into the salon to pick up a book, and
I noticed the clock."

"In other words, you and Vawdrey distinctly lingered here from about five minutes past ten till the hour you mention?"

"I don't know how distinct we were, but

we were very jolly. *Ou voulez-vous en venir ?*"
Blanche Adney asked.

"Simply to this, dear lady: that at the
time your companion was occupied in the
manner you describe, he was also engaged
in literary composition in his own room."

She stopped short at this, and her eyes
had an expression in the darkness. She
wanted to know if I challenged her verac-
ity; and I replied that, on the contrary, I
backed it up—it made the case so interesting. She returned that this would only be
if she should back up mine; which, however, I had no difficulty in persuading her
to do, after I had related to her circumstan-
tially the incident of my quest of the manuscript — the manuscript which, at the time,
for a reason I could now understand, appeared to have passed so completely out of
her own head.

"His talk made me forget it — I forgot I
sent you for it. He made up for his fiasco
in the salon: he declaimed me the scene,"
said my companion. She had dropped on a
bench to listen to me, and, as we sat there,
had briefly cross-examined me. Then she

broke out into fresh laughter. "Oh, the eccentricities of genius!"

"They seem greater even than I supposed."

"Oh, the mysteries of greatness!"

"You ought to know all about them, but they take me by surprise."

"Are you absolutely certain it was Mr. Vawdrey?" my companion asked.

"If it wasn't he, who in the world was it? That a strange gentleman, looking exactly like him, should be sitting in his room at that hour of the night and writing at his table *in the dark*," I insisted, "would be practically as wonderful as my own contention."

"Yes, why in the dark?" mused Mrs. Adney.

"Cats can see in the dark," I said.

She smiled at me dimly. "Did it look like a cat?"

"No, dear lady; but I'll tell you what it did look like — it looked like the author of Vawdrey's admirable works. It looked infinitely more like him than our friend does himself," I declared.

"Do you mean it was somebody he gets to do them?"

"Yes, while he dines out and disappoints you."

"Disappoints me?" murmured Mrs. Adney, artlessly.

"Disappoints *me*—disappoints every one who looks in him for the genius that created the pages they adore. Where is it in his talk?"

"Ah, last night he was splendid," said the actress.

"He's always splendid, as your morning bath is splendid, or a sirloin of beef, or the railway service to Brighton. But he's never rare."

"I see what you mean."

"That's what makes you such a comfort to talk to. I've often wondered—now I know. There are two of them."

"What a delightful idea!"

"One goes out, the other stays at home. One is the genius, the other's the bourgeois; and it's only the bourgeois whom we personally know. He talks, he circulates, he's awfully popular; he flirts with you—"

"Whereas it's the genius *you* are privileged to see!" Mrs. Adney broke in. "I'm much obliged to you for the distinction."

I laid my hand on her arm. "See him yourself. Try it, test it, go to his room."

"Go to his room? It wouldn't be proper!" she exclaimed, in the tone of her best comedy.

"Anything is proper in such an inquiry. If you see him, it settles it."

"How charming — to settle it!" She thought a moment, then she sprang up. "Do you mean *now ?*"

"Whenever you like."

"But suppose I should find the wrong one?" said Blanche Adney, with an exquisite effect.

"The wrong one? Which one do you call the right?"

"The wrong one for a lady to go and see. Suppose I shouldn't find—the genius?"

"Oh, I'll look after the other," I replied. Then, as I happened to glance about me, I added, "Take care, here comes Lord Mellifont."

" I wish you'd look after *him*," my inter-
locutress murmured.

"What's the matter with him ?"

" That's just what I was going to tell you."

" Tell me now; he's not coming."

Blanche Adney looked a moment. Lord
Mellifont, who appeared to have emerged
from the hotel to smoke a meditative cigar,
had paused, at a distance from us, and stood
admiring the wonders of the prospect, dis-
cernible even in the dusk. We strolled
slowly in another direction, and she presently said, "My idea is almost as droll as yours."

" I don't call mine droll ; it's beautiful."

" There's nothing so beautiful as the
droll," Mrs. Adney declared.

" You take a professional view. But I'm
all ears." My curiosity was indeed alive
again.

" Well then, my dear friend, if Clare
Vawdrey is double (and I'm bound to say I
think that the more of him the better), his
lordship there has the opposite complaint :
he isn't even whole."

We stopped once more, simultaneously.
" I don't understand."

"No more do I. But I have a fancy that if there are two of Mr. Vawdrey, there isn't so much as one, all told, of Lord Mellifont."

I considered a moment, then I laughed out. "I think I see what you mean!"

"That's what makes *you* a comfort. Did you ever see him alone?"

I tried to remember. "Oh yes; he has been to see me."

"Ah, then he wasn't alone."

"And I've been to see him, in his study."

"Did he know you were there?"

"Naturally—I was announced."

Blanche Adney glanced at me like a lovely conspirator. "You mustn't be announced!" With this she walked on.

I rejoined her, breathless. "Do you mean one must come upon him when he doesn't know it?"

"You must take him unawares. You must go to his room—that's what you must do."

If I was elated by the way our mystery opened out, I was also, pardonably, a little confused. "When I know he's not there?"

" When you know he *is*."

"And what shall I see?"

"You won't see anything!" Mrs. Adney cried as we turned round.

We had reached the end of the terrace, and our movement brought us face to face with Lord Mellifont, who, resuming his walk, had now, without indiscretion, overtaken us. The sight of him at that moment was illuminating, and it kindled a great backward train, connecting itself with one's general impression of the personage. As he stood there smiling at us and waving a practised hand into the transparent night (he introduced the view as if it had been a candidate and " supported " the very Alps), as he rose before us in the delicate fragrance of his cigar and all his other delicacies and fragrances, with more perfections, somehow, heaped upon his handsome head than one had ever seen accumulated before, he struck me as so essentially, so conspicuously and uniformly the public character that I read in a flash the answer to Blanche Adney's riddle. He was all public and had no corresponding private life, just as Clare

Vawdrey was all private and had no corresponding public one. I had heard only half my companion's story, yet as we joined Lord Mellifont (he had followed us—he liked Mrs. Adney; but it was always to be conceived of him that he accepted society rather than sought it), as we participated for half an hour in the distributed wealth of his conversation, I felt with unabashed duplicity that we had, as it were, found him out. I was even more deeply diverted by that whisk of the curtain to which the actress had just treated me than I had been by my own discovery; and if I was not ashamed of my share of her secret any more than of having divided my own with her (though my own was, of the two mysteries, the more glorious for the personage involved), this was because there was no cruelty in my advantage, but on the contrary an extreme tenderness and a positive compassion. Oh, he was safe with me, and I felt moreover rich and enlightened, as if I had suddenly put the universe into my pocket. I had learned what an affair of the spot and the moment a great appearance

may be. It would doubtless be too much
to say that I had always suspected the
possibility, in the background of his lordship's being, of some such beautiful instance; but it is at least a fact that, patroniz-
ing as it sounds, I had been conscious of a
certain reserve of indulgence for him. I
had secretly pitied him for the perfection
of his performance, had wondered what
blank face such a mask had to cover, what
was left to him for the immitigable hours in
which a man sits down with himself, or,
more serious still, with that intenser self,
his lawful wife. How was he at home, and
what did he do when he was alone? There
was something in Lady Mellifont that gave
a point to these researches—something that
suggested that even to her he was still the
public character, and that she was haunted
by similar questionings. She had never
cleared them up; that was her eternal
trouble. We therefore knew more than she
did, Blanche Adney and I; but we wouldn't
tell her for the world, nor would she probably thank us for doing so. She preferred
the relative grandeur of uncertainty. She

was not at home with him, so she couldn't
say ; and with her he was not alone, so he
couldn't show her. He represented to his
wife and he was a hero to his servants, and
what one wanted to arrive at was what
really became of him when no eye could
see. He rested, presumably ; but what
form of rest could repair such a plenitude
of presence ? Lady Mellifont was too
proud to pry, and as she had never looked
through a keyhole she remained dignified
and unassuaged.

It may have been a fancy of mine that
Blanche Adney drew out our companion, or
it may be that the practical irony of our
relation to him at such a moment made me
see him more vividly ; at any rate, he never
had struck me as so dissimilar from what
he would have been if we had not offered
him a reflection of his image. We were
only a concourse of two, but he had never
been more public. His perfect manner had
never been more perfect, his remarkable
tact had never been more remarkable. I
had a tacit sense that it would all be in
the morning papers, with a leader, and also

4

a secretly exhilarating one that I knew
something that wouldn't be, that never
could be, though any enterprising journal
would give one a fortune for it. I must
add, however, that in spite of my enjoyment—it was almost sensual, like that of a
consummate dish—I was eager to be alone
again with Mrs. Adney, who owed me an
anecdote. It proved impossible, that evening, for some of the others came out to see
what we found so absorbing; and then
Lord Mellifont bespoke a little music from
the fiddler, who produced his violin and
played to us divinely, on our platform of
echoes, face to face with the ghosts of the
mountains. Before the concert was over I
missed our actress, and glancing into the
window of the salon, saw that she was es-
tablished with Vawdrey, who was reading to
her from a manuscript. The great scene
had apparently been achieved, and was
doubtless the more interesting to Blanche
from the new lights she had gathered about
its author. I judged it discreet not to disturb them, and I went to bed without
seeing her again. I looked out for her be-

times the next morning, and as the promise
of the day was fair, proposed to her that we
should take to the hills, reminding her of
the high obligation she had incurred.   She
recognized the obligation and gratified me
with her company; but before we had
strolled ten yards up the pass she broke
out with intensity : " My dear friend, you've
no idea how it works in me!   I can think
of nothing else."

"Than your theory about Lord Mellifont ?"

"Oh, bother Lord Mellifont!   I allude
to yours about Mr. Vawdrey, who is much
the more interesting person of the two.
I'm fascinated by that vision of his—what-
do-you-call-it ?"

" His alternative identity ?"

" His other self ; that's easier to say."

" You accept it, then, you adopt it ?"

"Adopt it ?   I rejoice in it !   It became
tremendously vivid to me last evening."

" While he read to you there ?"

"Yes, as I listened to him, watched him.
It simplified everything, explained everything."

"That's indeed the blessing of it. Is the scene very fine?"

"Magnificent! and he reads beautifully."

"Almost as well as the other one writes!" I laughed.

This made my companion stop a moment, laying her hand on my arm. "You utter my very impression. I felt that he was reading me the work of another man."

"What a service to the other man!"

"Such a totally different person," said Mrs. Adney. We talked of this difference as we went on, and of what a wealth it constituted, what a resource for life, such a duplication of character.

"It ought to make him live twice as long as other people," I observed.

"Ought to make which of them?"

"Well, both; for after all they're members of a firm, and one of them couldn't carry on the business without the other. Moreover, mere survival would be dreadful for either."

Blanche Adney was silent a little; then she exclaimed: "I don't know—I wish he *would* survive!"

"May I, on my side, inquire which?"

"If you can't guess, I won't tell you."

"I know the heart of woman. You always prefer the other."

She halted again, looking round her. "Off here, away from my husband, I *can* tell you. I'm in love with him!"

"Unhappy woman, he has no passions," I answered.

"That's exactly why I adore him. Doesn't a woman with my history know that the passions of others are insupportable? An actress, poor thing, can't care for any love that's not all on *her* side; she can't afford to be repaid. My marriage proves that; marriage is ruinous. Do you know what was in my mind last night, all the while Mr. Vawdrey was reading me those beautiful speeches? An insane desire to see the author." And dramatically, as if to hide her shame, Blanche Adney passed on.

"We'll manage that," I returned. "I want another glimpse of him myself. But meanwhile please remember that I've been waiting more than forty-eight hours for the evidence that supports your sketch, intensely

suggestive and plausible, of Lord Mellifont's private life."

"Oh, Lord Mellifont doesn't interest
me."

"He did yesterday," I said.

"Yes, but that was before I fell in love.
You blotted him out with your story."

"You'll make me sorry I told it. Come,"
I pleaded, "if you don't let me know how
your idea came into your head I shall
imagine you simply made it up."

"Let me recollect, then, while we wander
in this grassy valley."

We stood at the entrance of a charming
crooked gorge, a portion of whose level
floor formed the bed of a stream that was
smooth with swiftness. We turned into it,
and the soft walk beside the clear torrent
drew us on and on; till suddenly, as we
continued and I waited for my companion
to remember, a bend of the valley showed
us Lady Mellifont coming towards us. She
was alone, under the canopy of her parasol,
drawing her sable train over the turf; and
in this form, on the devious ways, she was
a sufficiently rare apparition. She usually

took a footman, who marched behind her
on the highroads and whose livery was
strange to the mountaineers. She blushed
on seeing us, as if she ought somehow to
justify herself; she laughed vaguely, and
said she had come out for a little early
stroll. We stood together a moment, ex-
changing platitudes, and then she remarked
that she had thought she might find her
husband.

"Is he in this quarter?" I inquired.

"I supposed he would be. He came out
an hour ago to sketch."

"Have you been looking for him?" Mrs.
Adney asked.

"A little; not very much," said Lady
Mellifont.

Each of the women rested her eyes with
some intensity, as it seemed to me, on the
eyes of the other.

"We'll look for him *for* you, if you like,"
said Mrs. Adney.

"Oh, it doesn't matter. I thought I'd
join him."

"He won't make his sketch if you don't,"
my companion hinted.

"Perhaps he will if *you* do," said Lady Mellifont.

"Oh, I dare say he'll turn up," I interposed.

"He certainly will, if he knows we're here!" Blanche Adney retorted.

"Will you wait while we search?" I asked of Lady Mellifont.

She repeated that it was of no consequence; upon which Mrs. Adney went on: "We'll go into the matter for our own pleasure."

"I wish you a pleasant expedition," said her ladyship, and was turning away, when I sought to know if we should inform her husband that she had followed him. She hesitated a moment; then she jerked out, oddly, "I think you had better not." With this she took leave of us, floating a little stiffly down the gorge.

My companion and I watched her retreat, then we exchanged a stare, while a light ghost of a laugh rippled from the actress's lips. "She might be walking in the shrubberies at Mellifont!"

"She suspects it, you know," I replied.

"And she doesn't want him to know it. There won't be any sketch."

"Unless we overtake him," I subjoined. "In that case we shall find him producing one, in the most graceful attitude, and the queer thing is that it will be brilliant."

"Let us leave him alone; he'll have to come home without it."

"He'd rather never come home. Oh, he'll find a public!"

"Perhaps he'll do it for the cows," Blanche Adney suggested; and as I was on the point of rebuking her profanity she went on, "That's simply what I happened to discover."

"What are you speaking of?"

"The incident of day before yesterday."

"Ah, let's have it, at last!"

"That's all it was—that I was like Lady Mellifont; I couldn't find him."

"Did you lose him?"

"He lost *me*—that appears to be the way of it. He thought I was gone."

"But you did find him, since you came home with him."

"It was he who found *me*. That again is

what must happen. He's there from the moment he knows somebody else is."

" I understand his intermissions," I said, after a short reflection ; " but I don't quite seize the law that governs them."

" Oh, it's a fine shade, but I caught it at that moment. I had started to come home. I was tired, and I had insisted on his not coming back with me. We had found some rare flowers—those I brought home—and it was he who had discovered almost all of them. It amused him very much, and I knew he wanted to get more ; but I was weary and I quitted him. He let me go— where else would have been his tact ?—and I was too stupid then to have guessed that from the moment I was not there no flower would be gathered. I started homeward, but at the end of three minutes I found I had brought away his penknife—he had lent it to me to trim a branch—and I knew he would need it. I turned back a few steps to call him, but before I spoke I looked about for him. You can't understand what happened then without having the place before you."

"You must take me there," I said.

"We may see the wonder here. The place was simply one that offered no chance for concealment—a great gradual hill-side, without obstructions or trees. There were some rocks below me, behind which I myself had disappeared, but from which, on coming back, I immediately emerged again."

"Then he must have seen you."

"He was too utterly gone, for some reason best known to himself. It was probably some moment of fatigue—he's getting on, you know, so that, with the sense of returning solitude, the reaction had been proportionately great, the extinction proportionately complete. At any rate, the stage was as bare as your hand."

"Could he have been somewhere else?"

"He couldn't have been, in the time, anywhere but where I had left him. Yet the place was utterly empty—as empty as this stretch of valley before us. He had vanished—he had ceased to be. But as soon as my voice rang out (I uttered his name), he rose before me like the rising sun."

"And where did the sun rise?"

"Just where it ought to — just where he would have been, and where I should have seen him, had he been like other people."

I had listened with the deepest interest, but it was my duty to think of objections. "How long a time elapsed between the moment you perceived his absence and the moment you called?"

"Oh, only an instant. I don't pretend it was long."

"Long enough for you to be sure?" I said.

"Sure he wasn't there?"

"Yes; and that you were not mistaken, not the victim of some hocus-pocus of your eyesight?"

"I may have been mistaken, but I don't believe it. At any rate, that's just why I want you to look in his room."

I thought a moment. "How *can* I, when even his wife doesn't dare to?"

"She *wants* to; propose it to her. It wouldn't take much to make her. She does suspect."

I thought another moment. "Did he seem to know?"

"That I had missed him? So it struck
me, but he thought he had been quick
enough."

"Did you speak of his disappearance?"

"Heaven forbid! It seemed to me too
strange."

"Quite right. And how did he look?"

Trying to think it out again and reconsti-
tute her miracle, Blanche Adney gazed ab-
stractedly up the valley. Suddenly she exclaimed, "Just as he looks now!" and I
saw Lord Mellifont stand before us with his
sketch-block. I perceived, as we met him,
that he looked neither suspicious nor blank;
he looked simply, as he did always, everywhere, the principal feature of the scene.
Naturally he had no sketch to show us, but
nothing could better have rounded off our
actual conception of him than the way he
fell into position as we approached. He
had been selecting his point of view; he
took possession of it with a flourish of the
pencil. He leaned against a rock; his
beautiful little box of water-colors reposed
on a natural table beside him, a ledge of the
bank, which showed how inveterately nature

ministered to his convenience. He painted while he talked, and he talked while he painted; and if the painting was as miscellaneous as the talk, the talk would equally have graced an album. We waited while the exhibition went on, and it seemed indeed as if the conscious profiles of the peaks were interested in his success. They grew as black as silhouettes in paper, sharp against a livid sky, from which, however, there would be nothing to fear till Lord Mellifont's sketch should be finished. Blanche Adney communed with me dumbly, and I could read the language of her eyes: "Oh, if *we* could only do it as well as that! He fills the stage in a way that beats us." We could no more have left him than we could have quitted the theatre till the play was over; but in due time we turned round with him and strolled back to the inn, before the door of which his lordship, glancing again at his picture, tore the fresh leaf from the block and presented it, with a few happy words, to Mrs. Adney. Then he went into the house; and a moment later, looking up from where we stood, we saw him, above, at the window

of his sitting-room (he had the best apartments), watching the signs of the weather.

"He'll have to rest after this," Blanche
said, dropping her eyes on her water-color.

"Indeed he will!" I raised mine to the
window. Lord Mellifont had vanished.
"He's already reabsorbed."

"Reabsorbed?" I could see the actress
was now thinking of something else.

"Into the immensity of things. He has
lapsed again; there's an *entr'acte.*"

"It ought to be long." Mrs. Adney looked
up and down the terrace, and at that moment the head-waiter appeared in the door-
way. Suddenly she turned to this function-
ary with the question: "Have you seen
Mr. Vawdrey lately?"

The man immediately approached. "He
left the house five minutes ago—for a walk,
I think. He went down the pass; he had
a book."

I was watching the ominous clouds. "He
had better have had an umbrella."

The waiter smiled. "I recommended him
to take one."

"Thank you," said Mrs. Adney; and

the Oberkellner withdrew. Then she went
on, to me, abruptly, " Will you do me a
favor ?"

" Yes, if you'll do *me* one. Let me see if
your picture is signed."

She glanced at the sketch before giving
it to me. " For a wonder it isn't."

" It ought to be, for full value. May I
keep it awhile?"

" Yes, if you'll do what I ask. Take an
umbrella and go after Mr. Vawdrey."

" To bring him to Mrs. Adney ?"

" To keep him out—as long as you can."

" I'll keep him as long as the rain holds
off."

" Oh, never mind the rain !" my companion exclaimed.

" Would you have us drenched ?"

" Without remorse." Then, with a strange
light in her eyes, she added, " I'm going to
try."

" To try ?"

" To see the real one. Oh, if I can get
at him !" she broke out with passion.

" Try, try !" I replied. " I'll keep our
friend all day."

" If I can get at the one who does it "—
and she paused, with shining eyes—" if I can
have it out with him I shall get my part !"

" I'll keep Vawdrey forever !" I called
after her as she passed quickly into the
house.

Her audacity was communicative, and I
stood there in a glow of excitement. I
looked at Lord Mellifont's water-color and
I looked at the gathering storm ; I turned
my eyes again to his lordship's windows, and
then I bent them on my watch. Vawdrey
had so little the start of me that I should
have time to overtake him —time even if I
should take five minutes to go up to Lord
Mellifont's sitting-room (where we had all
been hospitably received), and say to him,
as a messenger, that Mrs. Adney begged he
would bestow upon his sketch the high con-
secration of his signature. As I again considered this work of art I perceived there
was something it certainly did lack : what
else then but so noble an autograph ? It
was my duty to suppy the deficiency without delay, and in accordance with this conviction I instantly re-entered the hotel. I

5

went up to Lord Mellifont's apartments; I
reached the door of his salon.   Here, however, I was met by a difficulty of which
my extravagance had not taken account.
If I were to knock I should spoil everything; yet was I prepared to dispense with
this ceremony?   I asked myself the question, and it embarrassed me; I turned my
little picture round and round, but it didn't
give me the answer I wanted.   I wanted
it to say: "Open the door gently, gently,
without a sound, yet very quickly; then you
will see what you will see."   I had gone so
far as to lay my hand upon the knob when
I became aware (having my wits so about
me), that exactly in the manner I was think-
of—gently, gently, without a sound—another door had moved, on the opposite side
of the hall.   At the same instant I found
myself smiling rather constrainedly upon
Lady Mellifont, who, on seeing me, had
checked herself on the threshold of her
room.   For a moment, as she stood there,
we exchanged two or three ideas that were
the more singular for being unspoken.   We
had caught each other hovering, and we un-

derstood each other; but as I stepped over
to her (so that we were separated from the
sitting-room by the width of the hall), her
lips formed the almost soundless entreaty,
"Don't!" I could see in her conscious eyes
everything that the word expressed—the
confession of her own curiosity and the dread
of the consequences of mine. "*Don't!*" she
repeated, as I stood before her. From the
moment my experiment could strike her as
an act of violence I was ready to renounce
it; yet I thought I detected in her frightened
face a still deeper betrayal—a possibility of
disappointment if I should give way. It
was as if she had said: "I'll let you do it,
if you'll take the responsibility. Yes, with
some one else, I'd surprise him. But it
would never do for him to think it was I."

"We soon found Lord Mellifont," I observed, in allusion to our encounter with
her an hour before, "and he was so good as
to give this lovely sketch to Mrs. Adney,
who has asked me to come up and beg him
to put in the omitted signature."

Lady Mellifont took the drawing from
me, and I could guess the struggle that

went on in her while she looked at it. She was silent for some time; then I felt that all her delicacies and dignities, all her old timidities and pieties were fighting against her opportunity. She turned away from me and with the drawing went back to her room. She was absent for a couple of minutes, and when she reappeared I could see that she had vanquished her temptation; that even, with a kind of resurgent horror, she had shrunk from it. She had deposited the sketch in the room. "If you will kindly leave the picture with me, I will see that Mrs. Adney's request is attended to," she said, with great courtesy and sweetness, but in a manner that put an end to our colloquy.

I assented, with a somewhat artificial enthusiasm perhaps, and then, to ease off our separation, remarked that we were going to have a change of weather.

"In that case we shall go—we shall go immediately," said Lady Mellifont. I was amused at the eagerness with which she made this declaration; it appeared to represent a coveted flight into safety, an escape with her threatened secret. I was the more surprised, therefore, when, as I was turning away, she put out her hand to take mine. She had the pretext of bidding me farewell, but as I shook hands with her on this supposition I felt that what the movement really conveyed was : " I thank you for the help you would have given me, but it's better as it is. If I should know, who would help me then?" As I went to my room to get my umbrella I said to myself, " She's sure, but she won't put it to the proof."

A quarter of an hour later I had overtaken Clare Vawdrey in the pass, and shortly after this we found ourselves looking for refuge. The storm had not only completely gathered, but it had broken at the last with extraordinary rapidity. We scrambled up a hill-side to an empty cabin, a rough structure that was hardly more than a shed for the protection of cattle. It was a tolerable shelter however, and it had fissures through which we could watch the splendid spectacle of the tempest. This entertainment lasted an hour—an hour that has remained with me as full of odd disparities. While the light-

ning played with the thunder and the rain
gushed in on our umbrellas, I said to myself that Clare Vawdrey was disappointing.
I don't know exactly what I should have
predicated of a great author exposed to the
fury of the elements, I can't say what particular Manfred attitude I should have expected my companion to assume, but it
seemed to me somehow that I shouldn't
have looked to him to regale me in such a
situation with stories (which I had already
heard) about the celebrated Lady Ring-
rose. Her ladyship formed the subject of
Vawdrey's conversation during this prodig-
ious scene, though before it was quite over
he had launched out on Mr. Chafer, the
scarcely less notorious reviewer. It broke
my heart to hear a man like Vawdrey talk
of reviewers. The lightning projected a
hard clearness upon the truth, familiar to
me for years, to which the last day or two
had added transcendent support—the irritating certitude that for personal relations
this admirable genius thought his second-
best good enough. It *was*, no doubt, as
society was made, but there was a contempt

in the distinction which could not fail to be
galling to an admirer. The world was vulgar and stupid, and the real man would
have been a fool to come out for it when
he could gossip and dine by deputy. None
the less my heart sank as I felt my
companion practice this economy. I don't
know exactly what I wanted; I suppose I
wanted him to make an exception for *me*.
I almost believed he would, if he had known
how I worshipped his talent. But I had
never been able to translate this to him,
and his application of his principle was re-
lentless. At any rate, I was more than
ever sure that at such an hour his chair at
home was not empty: *there* was the Manfred attitude, *there* were the responsive
flashes. I could only envy Mrs. Adney her
presumable enjoyment of them.

The weather drew off at last, and the rain
abated sufficiently to allow us to emerge
from our asylum and make our way back to
the inn, where we found on our arrival that
our prolonged absence had produced some
agitation. It was judged apparently that
the fury of the elements might have placed

us in a predicament. Several of our friends
were at the door, and they seemed a little
disconcerted when it was perceived that we
were only drenched. Clare Vawdrey, for
some reason. was wetter than I, and he
took his course to his room. Blanche Adney was among the persons collected to
look out for us, but as Vawdrey came towards her she shrank from him, without a
greeting; with a movement that I observed
as almost one of estrangement she turned
her back on him and went quickly into the
salon. Wet as I was, I went in after her;
on which she immediately flung round and
faced me. The first thing I saw was that
she had never been so beautiful. There
was a light of inspiration in her face, and
she broke out to me in the quickest whis-
per, which was at the same time the loudest
cry, I have ever heard: "I've got my *part!*"

"You went to his room—I was right?"

"Right?" Blanche Adney repeated. "Ah,
my dear fellow!" she murmured.

"He was there—you saw him?"

"He saw me. It was the hour of my
life!"

"It must have been the hour of his, if you were half as lovely as you are at this moment."

"He's splendid," she pursued, as if she didn't hear me. "He *is* the one who does it!" I listened, immensely impressed, and she added: "We understood each other."

"By flashes of lightning?"

"Oh, I didn't see the lightning then!"

"How long were you there?" I asked, with admiration.

"Long enough to tell him I adore him."

"Ah, that's what I've never been able to tell him!" I exclaimed, ruefully.

"I shall have my part—I shall have my part!" she continued, with triumphant indifference; and she flung round the room with the joy of a girl, only checking herself to say: "Go and change your clothes."

"You shall have Lord Mellifont's signature," I said.

"Oh, bother Lord Mellifont's signature! He's far nicer than Mr. Vawdrey," she went on, irrelevantly.

"Lord Mellifont?" I pretended to inquire.

"Confound Lord Mellifont!" And Blanche Adney, in her elation, brushed by me, whisking again through the open door. Just outside of it she came upon her husband; whereupon, with a charming cry of "We're talking of you, my love!" she threw herself upon him and kissed him.

I went to my room and changed my clothes, but I remained there till the evening. The violence of the storm had passed over us, but the rain had settled down to a drizzle. On descending to dinner I found that the change in the weather had already broken up our party. The Mellifonts had departed in a carriage and four, they had been followed by others, and several vehicles had been bespoken for the morning. Blanche Adney's was one of them, and on the pretext that she had preparations to make, she quitted us directly after dinner. Clare Vawdrey asked me what was the matter with her—she suddenly appeared to dislike him. I forget what answer I gave, but I did my best to comfort him by driving away with him the next day. Mrs. Adney had vanished when we came down; but they made up their quarrel in London, for he finished his play, which she produced. I must add that she is still, nevertheless, in want of the great part. I have a beautiful one in my head, but she doesn't come to see me to stir me up about it. Lady Mellifont always drops me a kind word when we meet, but that doesn't console me.

LORD BEAUPRÉ

I

Some reference had been made to North-
erley, which was within an easy drive, and
Firminger described how he had dined there
the night before and had found a lot of people. Mrs. Ashbury, one of the two visitors,
inquired who these people might be, and he
mentioned half a dozen names, among which
was that of young Raddle, which had been
a good deal on people's lips, and even in
the newspapers, on the occasion, still re-
cent, of his stepping into the fortune, exceptionally vast even as the product of a patent
glue, left him by a father whose ugly name
on all the vacant spaces of the world had
exasperated generations of men.

"Oh, is he there?" asked Mrs. Ashbury,
in a tone which might have been taken as a

vocal rendering of the act of pricking up one's ears. She didn't hand on the information to her daughter, who was talking—if a beauty of so few phrases could have been said to talk—with Mary Gosselin, but in the course of a few moments she put down her teacup with a failure of suavity, and, getting up, gave the girl a poke with her parasol. " Come, Maud, we must be stirring."

"You pay us a very short visit," said Mrs. Gosselin, intensely demure over the fine web of her knitting. Mrs. Ashbury looked hard for an instant into her bland eyes, then she gave poor Maud another poke. She alluded to a reason and expressed regrets ; but she got her daughter into motion, and Guy Firminger passed through the garden with the two ladies, to put them into their carriage. Mrs. Ashbury protested particularly against any further escort. While he was absent the other parent and child, sitting together on their pretty lawn in the yellow light of the August afternoon, talked of the frightful way Maud Ashbury had "gone off," and of something else as to

which there was more to say when their
third visitor came back.

"Don't think me grossly inquisitive if I
ask you where they told the coachman to
drive," said Mary Gosselin, as the young
man dropped near her into a low wicker
chair, stretching his long legs as if he had
been one of the family.

Firminger stared. "Upon my word, I
didn't particularly notice; but I think the
old lady said ' Home.'"

"There, mamma dear!" the girl exclaimed
triumphantly.

But Mrs. Gosselin only knitted on, per-
sisting in profundity. She replied that
"Home" was a feint, that Mrs. Ashbury
would already have given another order, and
that it was her wish to hurry off to North-
erley that had made her keep them from
going with her to the carriage, in which they
would have seen her take a suspected direction. Mary explained to Guy Firminger
that her mother had perceived poor Mrs.
Ashbury to be frantic to reach the house at
which she had heard that Mr. Raddle was
staying. The young man stared again, and

6

wanted to know what she desired to do with
Mr. Raddle. Mary replied that her mother
would tell him what Mrs. Ashbury desired
to do with poor Maud.

"What all Christian mothers desire," said
Mrs. Gosselin. "Only she doesn't know
how."

"To marry the dear child to Mr. Raddle," Mary added, smiling.

Firminger's vagueness expanded with the
subject. "Do you mean you want to marry
your dear child to that little cad?" he asked,
of the elder lady.

"I speak of the general duty—not of the
particular case," said Mrs. Gosselin.

"Mamma *does* know how," Mary went on.

"Then, why ain't you married?"

"Because we're not acting, like the Ashburys, with injudicious precipitation. Is
that correct?" the girl demanded, laughing,
of her mother.

"Laugh at me, my dear, as much as you
like—it's very lucky you've got me," Mrs.
Gosselin declared.

"She means I can't manage for myself,"
said Mary, to the visitor.

"What nonsense you talk!" Mrs. Gosselin murmured, counting stitches.

"I can't, mamma, I can't; I admit it," Mary continued.

"But injudicious precipitation and—what's the other thing?—creeping prudence, seem to come out in very much the same place," the young man objected.

"Do you mean since I too wither on the tree?"

"It only comes back to saying how hard it is nowadays to marry one's daughters," said the lucid Mrs. Gosselin, saving Firminger, however, the trouble of an ingenious answer. "I don't contend that, at the best, it's easy."

But Guy Firminger would not have struck you as capable of much conversational effort as he lounged there in the summer softness, with ironic familiarities, like one of the old friends who rarely deviate into sincerity. He was a robust but loose-limbed young man, with a well-shaped head and a face smooth, fair, and kind. He was in knickerbockers, and his clothes, which had seen service, were composed of articles that

didn't match. His laced boots were dusty
—he had evidently walked a certain distance; an indication confirmed by the
lingering, sociable way in which, in his
basket-seat, he tilted himself towards Mary
Gosselin. It pointed to a pleasant reason
for a long walk. This young lady, of five-
and-twenty, had black hair and blue eyes; a
combination often associated with the effect
of beauty. The beauty in this case, however, was dim and latent, not vulgarly obvious, and if her height and slenderness gave
that impression of length of line which, as
we know, is the fashion, Mary Gosselin had,
on the other hand, too much expression to
be generally admired. Every one thought
her intellectual; a few of the most simple-
minded even thought her plain. What Guy
Firminger thought—or rather what he took
for granted, for he was not built up on
depths of reflection—will probably appear
from this narrative.

"Yes, indeed; things have come to a pass
that's awful for *us*," the girl announced.

"For *us*, you mean," said Firminger.
"We're hunted like the ostrich; we're

trapped and stalked and run to earth. We go in fear—I assure you we do."

"Are *you* hunted, Guy?" Mrs. Gosselin asked, with an inflection of her own.

"Yes, Mrs. Gosselin, even *moi qui vous parle*, the ordinary male of commerce, inconceivable as it may appear. I know something about it."

"And of whom do you go in fear?" Mary Gosselin took up an uncut book and a paper-knife which she had laid down on the advent of the other visitors.

"My dear child, of Diana and her nymphs, of the spinster at large. She's always out with her rifle. And it isn't only that; you know there's always a second gun, a walking arsenal, at her heels. I forget, for the moment, who Diana's mother was, and the genealogy of the nymphs; but not only do the old ladies know the younger ones are out—they distinctly go *with* them."

"Who was Diana's mother, my dear?" Mrs. Gosselin inquired of her daughter.

"She was a beautiful old lady with pink ribbons in her cap and a genius for knitting," the girl replied, cutting her book.

"Oh, I'm not speaking of you two dears; you're not like any one else; you're an immense comfort," said Guy Firminger. "But they've reduced it to a science, and I assure you that if one were any one in particular, if one were not protected by one's obscurity, one's life would be a burden. Upon my honor, one wouldn't escape. I've seen it, I've watched them. Look at poor Beaupré—look at little Raddle over there. I object to him, but I bleed for him."

"Lord Beaupré won't marry again," said Mrs. Gosselin, with an air of conviction.

"So much the worse for him!"

"Come — that's a concession to our charms!" Mary laughed.

But the ruthless young man explained away his concession. "I mean that to be married 's the only protection—or else to be engaged."

"To be permanently engaged—wouldn't that do?" Mary Gosselin asked.

"Beautifully—I would try it if I were a *parti*."

"And how's the little boy?" Mrs. Gosselin presently inquired.

"What little boy?"

"Your little cousin — Lord Beaupré's child; isn't it a boy?"

"Oh, poor little beggar, he isn't up to much. He was awfully cut up by scarlet fever."

"You're not the rose indeed, but you're tolerably near it," the elder lady presently continued.

"What do you call near it? Not even in the same garden—not in any garden at all, alas!"

"There are three lives—but after all!"

"Dear lady, don't be homicidal!"

"What do you call the 'rose?'" Mary asked of her mother.

"The title," said Mrs. Gosselin, promptly but softly.

Something in her tone made Firminger laugh aloud. "You don't mention the property."

"Oh, I mean the whole thing."

"Is the property very large?" said Mary Gosselin.

"Fifty thousand a year," her mother responded; at which the young man laughed out again.

"Take care, mamma, or we shall be
thought to be out with our guns!" the girl
interposed; a recommendation that drew
from Guy Firminger the just remark that
there would be time enough for that when
his prospects should be worth speaking of.
He leaned over to pick up his hat and stick,
as if it were his time to go; but he didn't
go for another quarter of an hour, and during these minutes his prospects received
some frank consideration. He was Lord
Beaupré's first cousin, and the three inter-
vening lives were his lordship's own, that
of his little sickly son, and that of his uncle
the Major, who was also Guy's uncle, and
with whom the young man was at present
staying. It was from homely Trist, the
Major's house, that he had walked over to
Mrs. Gosselin's. Frank Firminger, who had
married in youth a woman with something
of her own, and eventually left the army, had
nothing but girls, but he was only of middle
age, and might possibly still have a son. At
any rate, his life was a very good one. Beaupré might marry again, and, marry or not,
he was barely thirty-three, and might live to

a great age. The child, moreover, poor little devil, would doubtless, with the growing consciousness of an incentive (there was none like feeling you were in people's way), develop a capacity for duration; so that altogether Guy professed himself, with the best will in the world, unable to take a rosy view of the disappearance of obstacles. He treated the subject with a jocularity that, in view of the remoteness of his chance, was not wholly tasteless, and the discussion, between old friends and in the light of this extravagance, was less crude than perhaps it sounds. The young man quite declined to see any latent brilliancy in his future. They had all been lashing him up, his poor dear mother, his uncle Frank, and Beaupré as well, to make that future political; but even if he should get in (he was nursing— oh, so languidly!—a possible opening), it would only be into the shallow edge of the stream. He would stand there like a tall idiot, with the water up to his ankles. He didn't know how to swim—in that element; he didn't know how to do anything.

"I think you're very perverse, my dear,"

said Mrs. Gosselin. " I'm sure you have great dispositions."

" For what—except for sitting here and talking with you and Mary? I revel in this sort of thing, but I scarcely like anything else."

" You'd do very well, if you weren't so lazy," Mary said. " I believe you're the very laziest person in the world."

" So do I—the very laziest in the world," the young man contentedly replied. " But how can I regret it, when it keeps me so quiet, when (I might even say) it makes me so amiable?"

" You'll have, one of these days, to get over your quietness, and perhaps even a little over your amiability," Mrs. Gosselin sagaciously stated.

" I devoutly hope not."

" You'll have to perform the duties of your position."

" Do you mean keep my stump of a broom in order and my crossing irreproachable?"

" You may say what you like; you will be a *parti*," Mrs. Gosselin continued.

"Well, then, if the worst comes to the worst, I shall do what I said just now : I shall get some good plausible girl to see me through."

" The proper way to 'get' her will be to marry her. After you're married you won't be a *parti*."

"Dear mamma, he'll think you're already levelling your rifle!" Mary Gosselin laughingly wailed.

Guy Firminger looked at her a moment. " I say, Mary, wouldn't *you* do ?"

"For the good plausible girl? Should I be plausible enough ?"

"Surely—what could be more natural? Everything would seem to contribute to the suitability of our alliance. I should be known to have known you for years—from childhood's sunny hour; I should be known to have bullied you, and even to have been bullied *by* you, in the period of pinafores. My relations from a tender age with your brother, which led to our school-room romps in holidays, and to the happy footing on which your mother has always been so good as to receive me here, would

add to all the presumptions of intimacy.
People would accept such a conclusion as
inevitable."

"Among all your reasons you don't mention the young lady's attractions," said
Mary Gosselin.

Firminger stared a moment, his clear
eye lighted by his happy thought. "I don't
mention the young man's. They would be
so obvious, on one side and the other, as
to be taken for granted."

"And is it your idea that one should pretend to be engaged to you all one's life?"

"Oh no; simply till I should have had
time to look round. I'm determined not
to be hustled and bewildered into matri-
mony — to be dragged to the shambles
before I know where I am. With such an
arrangement as the one I speak of I should
be able to take my time, to keep my head,
to make my choice."

"And how would the young lady make
hers?"

"How do you mean, hers?"

"The selfishness of men is something
exquisite. Suppose the young lady—if it's

conceivable that you should find one idiotic
enough to be a party to such a transaction
—suppose the poor girl herself should happen to wish to be *really* engaged?"

Guy Firminger thought a moment, with
his slow but not stupid smile. "Do you
mean to *me?*"

"To you—or to some one else."

"Oh, if she'd give me notice, I'd let her off."

"Let her off till you could find a substi-
tute?"

"Yes; but I confess it would be a great
inconvenience. People wouldn't take the
second one so seriously."

"She would have to make a sacrifice; she
would have to wait till you should know
where you were," Mrs. Gosselin suggested.

"Yes, but where would *her* advantage
come in?" Mary persisted.

"Only in the pleasure of charity; the
moral satisfaction of doing a fellow a good
turn," said Firminger.

"You must think people are keen to
oblige you!"

"Ah, but surely I could count on *you*,
couldn't I?" the young man asked.

Mary had finished cutting her book; she got up and flung it down on the tea-table. "What a preposterous conversation!" she exclaimed with force, tossing the words from her as she tossed her book; and, looking round her vaguely a moment, without meeting Guy Firminger's eyes, she walked away to the house.

Firminger sat watching her; then he said serenely to her mother: "Why has our Mary left us?"

"She has gone to get something, I suppose."

"What has she gone to get?"

"A little stick, to beat you, perhaps."

"You don't mean I've been objectionable?"

"Dear, no — I'm joking. One thing is very certain," pursued Mrs. Gosselin; "that you ought to work—to try to get on exactly as if nothing could ever happen. Oughtn't you?" She threw off the question mechanically as her visitor continued silent.

"I'm sure she doesn't like it!" he exclaimed, without heeding her appeal.

" Doesn't like what ?"

" My free play of mind. It's perhaps too much in the key of our old romps."

" You're very clever; she always likes *that*," said Mrs. Gosselin. " You ought to go in for something serious, for something honorable," she continued, " just as much as if you had nothing at all to look to."

" Words of wisdom, dear Mrs. Gosselin," Firminger replied, rising slowly from his relaxed attitude. " But what *have* I to look to ?"

She raised her mild, deep eyes to him as he stood before her—she might have been a fairy godmother. " Everything !"

" But you know I can't poison them !"

" That won't be necessary."

He looked at her an instant; then, with a laugh, " One might think *you* would undertake it !"

" I almost would—for *you*. Good-bye."

" Take care—if they *should* be carried off !" But Mrs. Gosselin only repeated her good-bye, and the young man departed before Mary had come back.

II

NEARLY two years after Guy Firminger had spent that friendly hour in Mrs. Gosselin's little garden in Hampshire this far-seeing woman was enabled (by the return of her son, who in New York, in an English bank, occupied a position in which they all rejoiced, to such great things might it possibly lead) to resume possession, for the season, of the little house in London which her husband had left her to live in, but which her native thrift, in determining her to let it for a term, had converted into a source of income. Hugh Gosselin, who was thirty years old, and at twenty three, before his father's death, had been despatched to America to exert himself, was understood to be doing very well—so well that his devotion to the interests of his employers had been rewarded, for the first time, with a real holiday. He was to remain in England from May to August, undertaking, as he said, to make it all right if during this time his mother should occupy (to contribute to his entertainment) the habitation in Chester Street. He was a small, preoccupied young man, with a sharpness as acquired as a new hat; he struck his mother and sister as intensely American. For the first few days after his arrival they were startled by his intonations, though they admitted that they had an escape when he reminded them that he might have brought with him an accent embodied in a wife.

"When you do take one," said Mrs. Gosselin, who regarded such an accident over there as inevitable, "you must charge her high for it."

It was not with this question, however, that the little family in Chester Street was mainly engaged, but with the last incident in the extraordinary succession of events which, like a chapter of romance, had in the course of a few months converted their vague and impecunious friend into a personage envied and honored. It was as if

7

a blight had been cast on all Guy Firminger's hinderances. On the day Hugh
Gosselin sailed from New York the delicate
little boy at Bosco had succumbed to an
attack of diphtheria. His father had died
of typhoid the previous winter at Naples;
his uncle, a few weeks later, had had a fatal
accident in the hunting-field. So strangely,
so rapidly had the situation cleared up, had
his fate and theirs worked for him. Guy
had opened his eyes one morning to an
earldom which carried with it a fortune not
alone nominally but really great. Mrs.
Gosselin and Mary had not written to him,
but they knew he was at Bosco; he had
remained there after the funeral of the
late little lord. Mrs. Gosselin, who heard
everything, had heard somehow that he was
behaving with the greatest consideration,
giving the guardians, the trustees, whatever
they were called, plenty of time to do
everything. Everything was comparatively
simple; in the absence of collaterals there
were so few other people concerned. The
principal relatives were poor Frank Firminger's widow and her girls, who had

seen themselves so near to new honors
and comforts. Probably the girls would
expect their cousin Guy to marry one of
them, and think it the least he could
decently do; a view the young man himself (if he were very magnanimous) might
possibly embrace. The question would be
whether he would be very magnanimous.
These young ladies exhausted in their three
persons the numerous varieties of plain-
ness. On the other hand, Guy Firminger—
or Lord Beaupré, as one would have to
begin to call him now—was unmistakably
kind. Mrs. Gosselin appealed to her son
as to whether their noble friend were not
unmistakably kind.

"Of course I've known him always, and
that time he came out to America — when
was it? four years ago—I saw him every
day. I like him awfully, and all that; but
since you push me, you know," said Hugh
Gosselin, "I'm bound to say that the first
thing to mention in any description of him
would be—if you wanted to be quite correct
—that he's unmistakably selfish."

"I see—I see," Mrs. Gosselin unblushingly replied. "Of course I know what you mean," she added, in a moment. "But is he any more so than any one else? Every one's unmistakably selfish."

"Every one but you and Mary," said the young man.

"And *you*, dear!" his mother smiled. "But a person may be kind, you know— mayn't he?—at the same time that he *is* selfish. There are different sorts."

"Different sorts of kindness?" Hugh Gosselin asked, with a laugh; and the inquiry undertaken by his mother occupied them for the moment, demanding a subtlety of treatment from which they were not conscious of shrinking, of which rather they had an idea that they were perhaps exceptionally capable. They came back to the temperate view that Guy would never put himself out, would probably never do anything great, but might show himself all the same a de- lightful member of society. Yes, he was probably selfish, like other people; but un- like most of them he was, somehow, ami- ably, attachingly, sociably, almost lovably selfish. Without doing anything great he

would yet be a great success—a big, pleasant,
gossiping, lounging, and, in its way, doubtless very splendid, presence. He would have
no ambition, and it was ambition that made
selfishness ugly. Hugh and his mother
were sure of this last point until Mary, before whom the discussion, when it reached
this stage, happened to be carried on, checked them by asking whether that, on the contrary, were not just what was supposed to
make it fine.

"Oh, he only wants to be comfortable,"
said her brother; "but he *does* want it !"

"There'll be a tremendous rush for him,"
Mrs. Gosselin prophesied to her son.

"Oh, he'll never marry. It will be too
much trouble."

" It's done here without any trouble—for
the men. One sees how long you've been
out of the country."

"There was a girl in New York whom he
might have married—he really liked her.
But he wouldn't turn round for her."

"Perhaps she wouldn't turn round for
him," said Mary.

"I dare say she'll turn round *now*," Mrs.

Gosselin rejoined; on which Hugh mentioned that there was nothing to be feared
from her, all her revolutions had been accomplished. He added that nothing would
make any difference—so intimate was his
conviction that Beaupré would preserve his
independence.

" Then I think he's not so selfish as you
say," Mary declared; " or, at any rate, one
will never know whether he is. Isn't married
life the great chance to show it ?"

" Your father never showed it," said Mrs.
Gosselin; and as her children were silent
in presence of this tribute to the departed, she added, smiling, " Perhaps you think
that *I* did !" They embraced her, to indi-
cate what they thought, and the conversation ended when she had remarked that
Lord Beaupré was a man who would be perfectly easy to manage *after* marriage, with
Hugh's exclaiming that this was doubtless
exactly why he wished to keep out of it.

Such was evidently his wish, as they were
able to judge in Chester Street when he
came up to town. He appeared there
oftener than was to have been expected, not

taking himself, in his new character, at all
too seriously to find stray half-hours for old
friends. It was plain that he was going to
do just as he liked, that he was not a bit
excited or uplifted by his change of fortune.
Mary Gosselin observed that he had no imagination—she even reproached him with
the deficiency to his face; an incident which
showed indeed how little seriously *she* took
him. He had no idea of playing a part, and
yet he would have been clever enough. He
wasn't even systematic about being simple;
his simplicity was a series of accidents and
indifferences. Never was a man more conscientiously superficial. There were matters
on which he valued Mrs. Gosselin's judg-
ment and asked her advice — without, as
usually appeared later, ever taking it; such
questions, mainly, as the claims of a prede-
cessor's servants, and those, in respect to
social intercourse, of the clergyman's family.
He didn't like his parson—what was a fellow
to do when he didn't like his parson?
What he did like was to talk with Hugh
about American investments, and it was
amusing to Hugh, though he tried not to

show his amusement, to find himself looking
at Guy Firminger in the light of capital.
To Mary he addressed from the first the
oddest snatches of confidential discourse,
rendered in fact, however, by the levity of
his tone, considerably less confidental than
in intention. He had something to tell her
that he joked about, yet without admitting
that it was any less important for being
laughable. It was neither more nor less
than that Charlotte Firminger, the eldest of
his late uncle's four girls, had designated to
him in the clearest manner the person she
considered he ought to marry. She appealed
to his sense of justice, she spoke and wrote,
or at any rate she looked and moved, she
sighed and sang, in the name of common
honesty. He had had four letters from her
that week, and to his knowledge there were
a series of people in London, people she
could bully, whom she had got to promise
to take her in for the season. She was going to be on the spot, she was going to follow him up. He took his stand on common
honesty, but he had a mortal horror of
Charlotte. At the same time, when a girl

had a jaw like that and had marked you—
really *marked* you, mind, you felt your safety
oozing away. He had given them during
the past three months, all those terrible girls,
every sort of present that Bond Street could
supply; but these demonstrations had only
been held to constitute another pledge.
Therefore what was a fellow to do? Besides,
there were other portents; the air was thick
with them, as the sky over battle-fields was
darkened by the flight of vultures. They
were flocking, the birds of prey, from every
quarter, and every girl in England, by Jove!
was going to be thrown at his head. What
had he done to deserve such a fate? He
wanted to stop in England and see all sorts
of things through; but how could he stand
there and face such a charge? Yet what
good would it do to bolt? Wherever he
should go there would be fifty of them there
first. On his honor he could say that he
didn't deserve it; he had never, to his own
sense, been a flirt, such a flirt at least as to
have given any one a handle. He appealed
candidly to Mary Gosselin to know whether
his past conduct justified such penalties.

"*Have* I been a flirt — have I given any one a handle?" he inquired, with pathetic intensity.

She met his appeal by declaring that he had been awful, committing himself right and left; and this manner of treating his affliction contributed to the sarcastic publicity (as regarded the little house in Chester Street) which presently became its natural element. Lord Beaupré's comical and yet thoroughly grounded view of his danger was soon a frequent theme among the Gosselins, who however had their own reasons for not communicating the alarm. They had no motive for concealing their interest in their old friend, but their allusions to him among their other friends may be said on the whole to have been studied. His state of mind recalled of course to Mary and her mother the queer talk about his prospects that they had had in the country that afternoon on which Mrs. Gosselin had been so strangely prophetic (she confessed that she had had a flash of divination : the future had been mysteriously revealed to her), and poor Guy, too, had seen himself quite as he was to be.

He had seen his nervousness, under inevitable pressure, deepen to a panic, and he now, in intimate hours, made no attempt to disguise that a panic had become his portion. It was a fixed idea with him that he should fall a victim to woven toils, be caught in a trap constructed with superior science. The science evolved in an enterprising age by this branch of industry, the manufacture of the trap matrimonial, he had terrible anecdotes to illustrate ; and what had he on his lips but a scientific term when he declared, as he perpetually did, that it was his fate to be hypnotized?

Mary Gosselin reminded him, they each in turn reminded him, that his safeguard was to fall in love; were he once to put himself under that protection, all of the mothers and maids in Mayfair would not prevail against him. He replied that this was just the impossibility ; it took leisure and calmness and opportunity and a free mind to fall in love, and never was a man less open to such experiences. He was literally fighting his way. He reminded the girl of his old fancy for pretending already to have disposed of his hand if he could put that hand on a young person who would like him well enough to be willing to participate in the fraud. She would have to place herself in rather a false position, of course—have to take a certain amount of trouble; but there would, after all, be a good deal of fun in it (there was always fun in duping the world) between the pair themselves, the two happy comedians.

"Why should they both be happy?" Mary Gosselin asked. "I understand why you should; but, frankly, I don't quite grasp the reason of *her* pleasure."

Lord Beaupré, with his sunny human eyes, thought a moment. "Why, for the lark, as they say, and that sort of thing. I should be awfully nice to her."

"She would require indeed to be in want of recreation!"

"Ah, but I should want a good sort—a quiet, reasonable one, you know!" he somewhat eagerly interposed.

"You're too delightful!" Mary Gosselin exclaimed, continuing to laugh. He thanked her for this appreciation, and she returned to her point—that she didn't really see the advantage his accomplice could hope to enjoy as her compensation for extreme disturbance.

Guy Firminger stared. " But what extreme disturbance ?"

" Why, it would take a lot of time; it might become intolerable."

" You mean I ought to pay her—to hire her for the season?"

Mary Gosselin considered him a moment. " Wouldn't marriage come cheaper at once?" she asked, with a quieter smile.

" You *are* chaffing me !" he sighed, forgivingly. " Of course she would have to be good-natured enough to pity me."

" Pity's akin to love. If she were good-natured enough to want to help you, she'd be good-natured enough to want to marry you. That would be *her* idea of help."

" Would it be *yours ?*" Lord Beaupré asked, rather eagerly.

" You're too absurd ! You must sail your own boat !" the girl answered, turning away.

That evening at dinner she stated to her companions that she had never seen a fatuity so dense, so serene, so preposterous as his lordship's.

"Fatuity, my dear! what do you mean?" her mother inquired.

"Oh, mamma, you know perfectly." Mary Gosselin spoke with a certain impatience.

"If you mean he's conceited, I'm bound to say I don't agree with you," her brother observed. "He's too indifferent to every one's opinion for that."

"He's not vain, he's not proud, he's not pompous," said Mrs. Gosselin.

Mary was silent a moment. "He takes more things for granted than any one I ever saw."

"What sort of things?"

"Well, one's interest in his affairs."

"With old friends surely a gentleman may."

"Of course," said Hugh Gosselin; "old friends have in turn the right to take for granted a corresponding interest on *his* part."

"Well, who could be nicer to us than he

is, or come to see us oftener?" his mother
asked.

"He comes exactly for the purpose I
speak of — to talk about himself," said
Mary.

"There are thousands of girls who would
be delighted with his talk," Mrs. Gosselin
returned.

" We agreed long ago that he's intensely
selfish," the girl went on; "and if I speak
of it to-day, it's not because that in itself is
anything of a novelty. What I'm freshly
struck with is simply that he more shame-
lessly shows it."

"He shows it, exactly," said Hugh; "he
shows all there is. There it is, on the
surface; there are not depths of it under-
neath."

"He's not hard," Mrs. Gosselin contend-
ed; "he's not impervious."

" Do you mean he's soft?" Mary asked.

" I mean he's yielding." And Mrs. Gosselin, with considerable expression, looked
across at her daughter. She added, before they rose from dinner, that poor
Beaupré had plenty of difficulties, and that

she thought, for her part, they ought in common loyalty to do what they could to assist him.

For a week nothing more passed between the two ladies on the subject of their noble friend, and in the course of this week they had the amusement of receiving in Chester Street a member of Hugh's American circle, Mr. Bolton-Brown, a young man from New York. He was a person engaged in large affairs, for whom Hugh Gosselin professed the highest regard, from whom in New York he had received much hospitality, and for whose advent he had from the first prepared his companions. Mrs. Gosselin begged the amiable stranger to stay with them, and if she failed to overcome his hesitation, it was because his hotel was near at hand and he should be able to see them often. It became evident that he would do so, and, to the two ladies, as the days went by, equally evident that no objection to such a relation was likely to arise. Mr. Bolton-Brown was delightfully fresh ; the most usual expressions acquired on his lips a wellnigh comical novelty, the

most superficial sentiments, in the look
with which he accompanied them, a really
touching sincerity. He was unmarried and
good-looking, clever and natural, and if he
was not very rich, was at least very free-
handed. He literally strewed the path of
the ladies in Chester Street with flowers, he
choked them with French confectionery.
Hugh, however, who was often rather mysterious on monetary questions, placed in a
light sufficiently clear the fact that his
friend had in Wall Street (they knew all
about Wall Street) improved each shining
hour. They introduced him to Lord Beaupré, who thought him "tremendous fun," as
Hugh said, and who immediately declared
that the four must spend a Sunday at
Bosco a week or two later. The date of
this visit was fixed—Mrs. Gosselin had
uttered a comprehensive acceptance; but
after Guy Firminger had taken leave of
them (this had been his first appearance
since the odd conversation with Mary), our
young lady confided to her mother that she
should not be able to join the little party.
She expressed the conviction that it would

8

be all that was essential if Mrs. Gosselin
should go with the two others. On being
pressed to communicate the reason of this
aloofness, Mary was able to give no better
one than that she never had cared for
Bosco.

" What makes you hate him so?" her
mother presently broke out, in a tone which
brought the red to the girl's cheek. Mary
denied that she entertained for Lord Beaupré any sentiment so intense; to which
Mrs. Gosselin rejoined, with some stern·
ness and, no doubt, considerable wisdom:
" Look out what you do, then, or you'll be
thought by every one to be in love with
him!"

III

I KNOW not whether it was this danger—
that of appearing to be moved to extremes
—that weighed with Mary Gosselin; at any
rate, when the day, arrived she had decided
to be perfectly colorless and take her
share of Lord Beaupré's hospitality. On

perceiving that the house, when with her companions she reached it, was full of visitors, she consoled herself with the sense that such a share would be of the smallest. She even wondered whether its smallness might not be caused in some degree by the sufficiently startling presence, in this stronghold of the single life, of Maud Ashbury and her mother. It was true that during the Saturday evening she never saw their host address an observation to them; but she was struck, as she had been struck before, with the girl's cold and magnificent beauty. It was very well to say she had "gone off;" she was still handsomer than any one else. She had failed in everything she had tried; the campaign undertaken with so much energy against young Raddle had been conspicuously disastrous. Young Raddle had married his grandmother, or a person who might have filled such an office, and Maud was a year older, a year more disappointed, and a year more ridiculous. Nevertheless one could scarcely believe that a creature with such advantages would always fail, though, indeed, the poor girl was stupid enough to be a warning. Perhaps it would be at Bosco, or with the master of Bosco, that fate had appointed her to succeed. Except Mary herself, she was the only young unmarried woman on the scene, and Mary glowed with the generous sense of not being a competitor. She felt as much out of the question as the blooming wives, the heavy matrons, who formed the rest of the female contingent. Before the evening closed, however, her host, who, she saw, was delightful in his own house, mentioned to her that he had a couple of guests who had not been invited.

" Not invited?"

" They drove up to my door as they might have done to an inn. They asked for rooms, and complained of those that were given them. Don't pretend not to know who they are."

" Do you mean the Ashburys? How amusing!"

" Don't laugh; it freezes my blood."

" Do you really mean you're afraid of them ?"

" I tremble like a leaf. Some monstrous

ineluctable fate seems to look at me out of
their eyes."

"That's because you secretly admire
Maud. How can you help it? She's extremely good-looking, and if you get rid of
her mother, she'll become a very nice girl."

"It's an odious thing, no doubt, to say
about a young person under one's own roof,
but I don't think I ever saw any one who
happened to be less to my taste," said Guy
Firminger. "I don't know why I don't turn
them out even now."

Mary persisted in sarcasm. "Perhaps
you can make her have a worse time by
letting her stay."

"*Please* don't laugh," her interlocutor
repeated. "Such a fact as I have mentioned to you seems to me to speak volumes
—to show you what my life is."

"Oh, your life, your life!" Mary Gosselin
murmured, with her mocking note.

"Don't you agree that at such a rate it
may easily become impossible?"

"Many people would change with you. I
don't see what there is for you to do but to
bear your cross!"

"That's easy talk!" Lord Beaupré sighed.

"Especially from me, do you mean? How do you know I don't bear mine?"

"Yours?" he asked, vaguely.

"How do you know that *I'm* not persecuted, that *my* footsteps are not dogged, that *my* life isn't a burden?"

They were walking in the old gardens, the proprietor of which, at this, stopped short. "Do you mean by fellows who want to marry you?"

His tone produced on his companion's part an irrepressible peal of hilarity; but she walked on as she exclaimed: "You speak as if there couldn't *be* such madmen!"

"Of course such a charming girl must be made up to," Guy Firminger conceded as he overtook her.

"I don't speak of it; I keep quiet about it."

"You realize then, at any rate, that it's all horrid when you don't care for them."

"I suffer in silence, because I know there are worse tribulations. It seems to me you ought to remember that," Mary continued. "Your cross is small compared with your crown. You've everything in the world that most people most desire, and I'm bound to say I think your life is made very comfortable for you. If you're oppressed by the quantity of interest and affection you inspire, you ought simply to make up your mind to bear up and be cheerful under it."

Lord Beaupré received this admonition with perfect good-humor; he professed himself able to do it full justice. He remarked that he would gladly give up some of his material advantages to be a little less badgered, and that he had been quite content with his former insignificance. No doubt, however, such annoyances were the essential drawbacks of ponderous promotions; one had to pay for everything. Mary was quite right to rebuke him; her own attitude, as a young woman much admired, was a lesson to his irritability. She cut this appreciation short, speaking of something else; but a few minutes later he broke out irrelevantly: "Why, if you are hunted as well as I, that dodge I proposed

to you would be just the thing for us *both!*"
He had evidently been reasoning it out.

Mary Gosselin was silent at first, she only
paused gradually in their walk at a point
where four long alleys met. In the centre
of the circle, on a massive pedestal, rose in
Italian bronze a florid, complicated image,
so that the place made a charming Old
World picture. The grounds of Bosco were
stately without stiffness and full of marble
terraces and misty avenues. The fountains
in particular were royal. The girl had told
her mother in London that she disliked this
fine residence, but she now looked round
her with a vague, pleased, sigh, holding up
her glass (she had been condemned to wear
one, with a long handle, since she was fif-
teen), to consider the weather-stained garden group. "What a perfect place of its
kind!" she musingly exclaimed.

"Wouldn't it really be just the thing?"
Lord Beaupré went on, with the eagerness
of his idea.

"Wouldn't what be just the thing?"

"Why, the defensive alliance we've already talked of. You wanted to know the

good it would do *you*. Now you see the
good it would do you!"

"I don't like practical jokes," said Mary.
"The remedy's worse than the disease,"
she added; and she began to follow one of
the paths that took the direction of the
house.

Poor Lord Beaupré was absurdly in love
with his invention; he had all an inventor's
importunity. He kept up his attempt to
place his "dodge" in a favorable light, in
spite of a further objection from his companion, who assured him that it was one of
those contrivances which break down in
practice in just the proportion in which they
make a figure in theory. At last she said:
"I was not sincere just now when I told
you I'm worried. I'm *not* worried!"

"They *don't* buzz about you?" Guy Firminger asked.

She hesitated an instant. "They buzz
about me; but at bottom it's flattering, and
I don't mind it. Now please drop the subject."

He dropped the subject, though not without congratulating her on the fact that,

unlike his infirm self, she could keep her head and her temper. His infirmity found a trap laid for it before they had proceeded twenty yards, as was proved by his sudden exclamation of horror. " Good heavens — if there isn't Lottie !"

Mary perceived, in effect, in the distance a female figure coming towards them over a stretch of lawn, and she simultaneously saw, as a gentleman passed from behind a clump of shrubbery, that it was not unattended. She recognized Charlotte Firminger, and she also distinguished the gentleman. She was moved to larger mirth at the dismay expressed by poor Firminger, but she was able to articulate: "Walking with Mr. Brown !"

Lord Beauprê stopped again before they were joined by the pair. "Does *he* buzz about you ?"

"Mercy, what questions you ask !" his companion exclaimed.

"Does he—*please?*" the young man repeated, with odd intensity.

Mary looked at him an instant; she was puzzled by the deep annoyance that had

flushed through the essential good-humor
of his face. Then she saw that this annoyance had exclusive reference to poor Charlotte ; so that it left her free to reply, with
another laugh : "Well, yes—he does. But
you know I like it !"

"I don't, then !" Before she could have
asked him, even had she wished to, in what
manner such a circumstance concerned him,
he added, with his droll agitation: "I never
invited *her*, either ! Don't let her get at
me !"

"What can I do ?" Mary demanded, as
the others advanced.

"Please take her away, keep her yourself ! I'll take the American, I'll keep *him*,"
he murmured, inconsequently, as a bribe.

"But I don't object to him."

"Do you like him so much ?"

"Very much indeed," the girl replied.

The reply was perhaps lost upon her interlocutor, whose eye now fixed itself gloom-
ily on the dauntless Charlotte. As Miss
Firminger came nearer he exclaimed, almost
loud enough for her to hear, "I think I
shall *murder* her some day !"

Mary Gosselin's first impression had
been that, in his panic, under the empire
of that fixed idea to which he confessed
himself subject, he attributed to his kins-
woman machinations and aggressions of
which she was incapable; an impression
that might have been confirmed by this
young lady's decorous placidity, her pas-
sionless eyes, her expressionless cheeks, and
colorless tones. She was ugly, yet she
was orthodox ; she was not what writers of
books called intense. But after Mary, to
oblige their host, had tried, successfully
enough, to be crafty, had drawn her on to
stroll a little in advance of the two gentlemen, she became promptly aware, by the
mystical influence of propinquity, that Miss
Firminger was indeed full of views, of a
purpose single, simple, and strong, which
gave her the effect of a person carrying with
a stiff, steady hand, with eyes fixed and lips
compressed, a cup charged to the brim.
She had driven over to lunch, driven from
somewhere in the neighborhood; she had
picked up some weak woman as an escort.
Mary, though she knew the neighborhood,

failed to recognize her base of operations;
and as Charlotte was not specific, ended
by suspecting that, far from being entertained by friends, she had put up at an inn
and hired a fly. This suspicion startled her;
it gave her for the first time something of the
measure of the passions engaged, and she
wondered to what the insecurity complained
of by Guy might lead. Charlotte on arriv-
ing had gone through a part of the house in
quest of its master (the servants being unable to tell her where he was), and she had
finally come upon Mr. Bolton-Brown, who
was looking at old books in the library. He
had placed himself at her service, as if he
had been trained immediately to recognize
in such a case his duty, and informing her
that he believed Lord Beaupré to be in
the grounds, had come out with her to help
to find him. Lottie Firminger questioned
her companion about this accommodating
person; she intimated that he was rather
odd but rather nice. Mary mentioned to
her that Lord Beaupré thought highly of
him; she believed they were going somewhere together. At this Miss Firminger

turned round to look for them, but they
had already disappeared, and the girl became ominously dumb.

Mary wondered afterwards what profit
she could hope to derive from such pro-
ceedings; they struck her own sense, naturally, as disreputable and desperate. She
was equally unable to discover the compensation they offered, in another variety,
to poor Maud Ashbury, whom Lord Beaupré, the greater part of the day, neglected
as conscientiously as he neglected his
cousin. She asked herself if he should be
blamed, and replied that the others should
be blamed first. He got rid of Charlotte
somehow after tea ; she had to fall back
to her mysterious lines. Mary knew this
method would have been detestable to him
—he hated to force his friendly nature ; she
was sorry for him and wished to lose sight
of him. She wished not to be mixed up,
even indirectly, with his tribulations, and
the fevered faces of the Ashburys were
particularly dreadful to her. She spent as
much of the long summer afternoon as
possible out of the house, which, indeed,

on such an occasion, emptied itself of most
of its inmates. Mary Gosselin asked her
brother to join her in a devious ramble;
she might have had other society, but she
was in a mood to prefer his. These two
were "great chums," and they had been
separated so long that they had arrears of
talk to make up. They had been at Bosco
more than once, and though Hugh Gosselin
said that the land of the free (which he had
assured his sister was even more enslaved
than dear old England) made one forget
there were such spots on earth, they both
remembered, a couple of miles away, a little
ancient church to which the walk across the
fields would be the right thing. They
talked of other things as they went, and
among them they talked of Mr. Bolton-
Brown, in regard to whom Hugh, as scant-
ily addicted to enthusiasm as to bursts of
song (he was determined not to be taken
in), became in commendation almost lyrical.
Mary asked what he had done with his
paragon, and he replied that he believed
him to have gone out stealthily to sketch;
they might come across him. He was ex-

traordinarily clever at water - colors, but
haunted with the fear that the public practice of such an art on Sunday was viewed
with disfavor in England. Mary exclaimed
that this was the respectable fact; and when
her brother ridiculed the idea, she told him
she had already noticed he had lost all
sense of things at home, so that Mr. Bolton-
Brown was apparently a better Englishman
than he. "He is indeed—he's awfully artificial!" Hugh returned; but it must be added that in spite of this rigor their American
friend, when they reached the goal of their
walk, was to be perceived in an irregular
attitude in the very church-yard. He was
perched on an old flat tomb, with a box of
colors beside him and a sketch half com-
pleted. Hugh asserted that this exercise
was the only thing that Mr. Bolton-Brown
really cared for, but the young man protested against the imputation in the face of
an achievement so modest. He showed his
sketch to Mary, however, and it consoled
her for not having kept up her own experiments; she never could make her trees so
leafy. He had found a lovely bit on the

other side of the hill, a bit he should like
to come back to, and he offered to show it
to his friends. They were on the point of
starting with him to look at it when Hugh
Gosselin, taking out his watch, remembered
the hour at which he had promised to be at
the house again to give his mother, who
wanted a little mild exercise, his arm. His
sister at this said she would go back with
him; but Bolton - Brown interposed an earnest inquiry. Mightn't she let Hugh keep
his appointment and let *him* take her over
the hill and bring her home?

" Happy thought—*do* that!" said Hugh,
with a crudity that showed the girl how completely he had lost his English sense. He
perceived, however, in an instant, that she
was embarrassed, whereupon he went on :
" My dear child, I've walked with girls so
often in America that we really ought to let
poor Brown walk with one in England." I
know not if it was the effect of this plea
or that of some further eloquence of their
friend; at any rate, Mary Gosselin in the
course of another minute had accepted the
accident of Hugh's secession, had seen him

9

depart with an injunction to her to render it clear to poor Brown that he had made quite a monstrous request. As she went over the hill with her companion she reflected that, since she had granted the request, it was not in her interest to pretend she had gone out of her way. She wondered, moreover, whether her brother had wished to throw them together; it suddenly occurred to her that the whole incident might have been prearranged. The idea made her a little angry with Hugh; it led her however to entertain no resentment against the other party (if party Mr. Brown had been) to the transaction. He told her all the delight that certain sweet old corners of rural England excited in his mind, and she liked him for hovering near some of her own secrets.

Hugh Gosselin meanwhile, at Bosco, strolling on the terrace with his mother, who preferred walks that were as slow as conspiracies, and had had much to say to him about his extraordinary indiscretion, repeated over and over (it ended by irritating her), that as he himself had been out for hours with

American girls, it was only fair to let their friend have a turn with an English one.

" Pay as much as you like, but don't pay with your sister !" Mrs. Gosselin replied; while Hugh submitted that it was just his sister who was required to make the payment *his.* She turned his logic to easy scorn, and she waited on the terrace till she had seen the two explorers reappear. When the ladies went to dress for dinner she expressed to her daughter her extreme disapproval of such conduct, and Mary did nothing more to justify herself than to exclaim at first, " Poor dear man !" and then to say, " I was afraid you wouldn't like it." There were reservations in her silence that made Mrs. Gosselin uneasy, and she was glad that at dinner Mr. Bolton-Brown had to take in Mrs. Ashbury ; it served him so right. This arrangement had, in Mrs. Gosselin's eyes, the added merit of serving Mrs. Ashbury right. She was more uneasy than ever when, after dinner, in the drawing-room, she saw Mary sit for a period on the same small sofa with the culpable American. This young couple leaned back together

familiarly, and their conversation had the
air of being desultory without being in the
least difficult. At last she quitted her place
and went over to them, remarking to Mr.
Bolton-Brown that she wanted him to come
and talk a bit to *her*. She conducted him
to another part of the room, which was vast
and animated by scattered groups, and held
him there very persuasively, quite mater-
nally, till the approach of the hour at which
the ladies would exchange looks and mur-
mur good-nights. She made him talk about
America, though he wanted to talk about
England, and she judged that she gave him
an impression of the kindest attention,
though she was really thinking, in alterna-
tion, of three important things. One of
these was a circumstance of which she had
become conscious only just after sitting
down with him — the prolonged absence of
Lord Beaupré from the drawing - room ;
the second was the absence, equally marked
(to her imagination), of Maud Ashbury, the
third was a matter different altogether.
" England gives one such a sense of im-
memorial continuity, something that drops

like a plummet-line into the past," said the young American, ingeniously exerting himself, while Mrs. Gosselin, rigidly contemporaneous, strayed into deserts of conjecture. Had the fact that their host was out of the room any connection with the fact that the most beautiful, even though the most suicidal, of his satellities had quitted it? Yet if poor Guy was taking a turn by starlight on the terrace with the misguided girl, what had he done with his resentment at her invasion, and by what inspiration of despair had Maud achieved such a triumph? The good lady studied Mrs. Ashbury's face across the room; she decided that triumph, accompanied perhaps with a shade of nervousness, looked out of her insincere eyes. An intelligent consciousness of ridicule was at any rate less present in them than ever. While Mrs. Gosselin had her infallible finger on the pulse of the occasion, one of the doors opened to readmit Lord Beaupré, who struck her as pale, and who immediately approached Mrs. Ashbury with a remark evidently intended for herself alone. It led this lady to rise with a movement of dismay

and, after a question or two, leave the room.
Lord Beaupré left it again in her company.
Mr. Bolton-Brown had also noticed the incident; his conversation languished, and he
asked Mrs. Gosselin if she supposed anything had happened. She turned it over a
moment, and then she said: "Yes, something will have happened to Miss Ashbury."

"What do you suppose? Is she ill?"

"I don't know; we shall see. They're
capable of anything."

"Capable of anything?"

"I've guessed it—she wants to have a
grievance."

"A grievance?" Mr. Bolton-Brown was
mystified.

"Of course you don't understand; how
should you? Moreover, it doesn't signify.
But I'm so vexed with them (he's a very old
friend of ours) that really, though I dare
say I'm indiscreet, I can't speak civilly of
them."

"Miss Ashbury's a wonderful type," said
the young American.

This remark appeared to irritate his companion. "I see perfectly what has happened ; she has made a scene."

"A scene?" Mr. Bolton - Brown was terribly out of it.

"She has tried to be injured—to provoke him, I mean, to some act of impatience, to some failure of temper, of courtesy. She has asked him if he wishes her to leave the house at midnight, and he may have answered— But no, he wouldn't !" Mrs. Gosselin suppressed the wild supposition.

"How you read it ! She looks so quiet."

"Her mother has coached her, and—I won't pretend to say *exactly* what has happened—they've done, somehow, what they wanted ; they've got him to do something to them that he'll have to make up for."

"What 'an evolution of ingenuity !" the young man laughed.

"It often answers."

"Will it in this case ?"

Mrs. Gosselin was silent a moment. "It *may.*"

"Really, you think ?"

"I mean it might, if it weren't for something else."

"I'm too judicious to ask what that is."

"I'll tell you when we're back in town," said Mrs. Gosselin, getting up.

Lord Beaupré was restored to them, and the ladies prepared to withdraw. Before she went to bed Mrs. Gosselin asked him if there had been anything the matter with Maud, to which he replied, with abysmal blankness (she had never seen him wear just that face), that he was afraid Miss Ashbury was ill. She proved, in fact, in the morning too unwell to return to London; a piece of news communicated to Mrs. Gosselin at breakfast.

"She'll have to stay; I can't turn her out of the house," said Guy Firminger.

"Very well; let her stay her fill!"

"I wish you would stay, too," the young man went on.

"Do you mean to nurse her?"

"No, her mother must do that. I mean to keep me company."

"*You?* You're not going up?"

"I think I had better wait over to-day, or long enough to see what's the matter."

"Don't you *know* what's the matter?"

He was silent a moment. "I may have been nasty last night."

"You have compunctions? You're too good-natured."

"I dare say I hit rather wild. It will look better for me to stop over twenty-four hours."

Mrs. Gosselin fixed her eyes on a distant object. "Let no one ever say you're selfish!"

"*Does* any one ever say it?"

"You're too generous, you're too soft, you're too foolish. But if it will give you any pleasure, Mary and I will wait till to-morrow."

"And Hugh, too, won't he, and Bolton-Brown?"

"Hugh will do as he pleases. But don't keep the American."

"Why not? He's all right."

"That's why I want him to go," said Mrs. Gosselin, who could treat a matter with candor, just as she could treat it with humor, at the right moment.

The party at Bosco broke up, and there was a general retreat to town. Hugh Gos-

selin pleaded pressing business, he accompanied the young American to London.
His mother and sister came back on the
morrow, and Bolton-Brown went in to see
them, as he often did, at tea-time.   He
found Mrs. Gosselin alone in the drawing-
room, and she took such a convenient occasion to mention to him, what she had
withheld on the eve of their departure from
Bosco, the reason why poor Maud Ashbury's
frantic assault on the master of that property
would be vain.   He was greatly surprised,
the more so that Hugh hadn't told him.
Mrs. Gosselin replied that Hugh didn't
know : she had not seen him all day, and it
had only just come out.   Hugh's friend, at
any rate, was deeply interested, and his interest took for several minutes the form of
throbbing silence.   At last Mrs. Gosselin
heard a sound below, on which she said,
quickly: "That's Hugh—I'll tell him now!"
She left the room with the request that their
visitor would wait for Mary, who would be
down in a moment.   During the instants
that he spent alone the visitor lurched, as
if he had been on a deck in a blow, to the

window, and stood there with his hands in
his pockets, staring vacantly into Chester
Street; then, turning away, he gave himself,
with an odd ejaculation, an impatient shake
which had the effect of enabling him to
meet Mary Gosselin composedly enough
when she came in. It took her mother
apparently some time to communicate the
news to Hugh, so that Bolton-Brown had a
considerable margin for nervousness and
hesitation before he could say to the girl,
abruptly, but with an attempt at a voice
properly gay: " You must let me very
heartily congratulate you !"

Mary stared. " On what ?"

" On your engagement."

" My engagement ?"

" To Lord Beaupré."

Mary Gosselin looked strange ; she colored. " Who told you I'm engaged ?"

" Your mother—just now."

" Oh !" the girl exclaimed, turning away.
She went and rang the bell for fresh tea,
rang it with noticeable force. But she said
" Thank you very much !" before the servant
came.

IV

Bolton-Brown did something that evening towards disseminating the news; he told it to the first people he met socially after leaving Chester Street; and this although he had to do himself a certain violence in speaking. He would have preferred to hold his peace; therefore if he resisted his inclination it was for an urgent purpose. This purpose was to prove to himself that he didn't mind. A perfect indifference could be for him the only result of any understanding Mary Gosselin might arrive at with any one, and he wanted to be more and more conscious of his indifference. He was aware, indeed, that it required demonstration, and this was why he was almost feverishly active. He could mentally concede at least that he had been surprised, for he had suspected nothing at Bosco. When a fellow was attentive in America

every one knew it, and judged by this stand-
ard Lord Beaupré made no show; how
otherwise should *he* have achieved that
sweet accompanied ramble? Everything, at
any rate, was lucid now, except, perhaps, a
certain ambiguity in Hugh Gosselin, who,
on coming into the drawing-room with his
mother, had looked flushed and grave, and
had stayed only long enough to kiss Mary
and go out again. There had been nothing
effusive in the scene; but then there was
nothing effusive in any English scene. This
helped to explain why Miss Gosselin had
been so blank during the minutes she spent
with him before her mother came back.

He himself wanted to cultivate tranquillity,
and he felt that he did so the next day in
not going again to Chester Street. He
went instead to the British Museum, where
he sat quite like an elderly gentleman, with
his hands crossed on the top of his stick
and his eyes fixed on an Assyrian bull.
When he came away, however, it was with
the resolution to move briskly; so that he
walked westward the whole length of Oxford
Street and arrived at the Marble Arch. He

stared for some minutes at this monument, as in the national collection he had stared at even less intelligible ones; then brushing away the apprehension that he should meet two persons riding together, he passed into the park. He didn't care a straw whom he met. He got upon the grass and made his way to the southern expanse, and when he reached the Row he dropped into a chair, rather tired, to watch the capering procession of riders. He watched it with a lustreless eye, for what he seemed mainly to extract from it was a vivification of his disappointment. He had had a hope that he should not be forced to leave London without inducing Mary Gosselin to ride with him; but that prospect failed, for what he had accomplished in the British Museum was the determination to go to Paris. He tried to think of the attractions supposed to be evoked by that name, and while he was so engaged he recognized that a gentleman on horseback, close to the barrier of the Row, was making a sign to him. The gentleman was Lord Beaupré, who had pulled up his horse, and whose sign the young

American lost no time in obeying. He went forward to speak to his late host, but during the instant of the transit he was able both to observe that Mary Gosselin was not in sight and to ask himself why she was not. She rode with her brother; why then didn't she ride with her future husband? It was singular at such a moment to see her future husband disporting himself alone. This personage conversed a few moments with Bolton-Brown, said it was too hot to ride, but that he ought to be mounted (*he* would give him a mount, if he liked), and was on the point of turning away when his interlocutor succumbed to the temptation to put his modesty to the test.

"Good-bye, but let me congratulate you first," said Bolton-Brown.

"Congratulate me? On what?" His look, his tone were very much what Mary Gosselin's had been.

" Why, on your engagement. Haven't you heard of it?"

Lord Beaupré stared a moment while his horse shifted uneasily. Then he laughed and said: " Which of them do you mean?"

"There's only one I know anything about. To Miss Gosselin," Brown added, after a puzzled pause.

"Oh yes, I see—thanks so much!" With this, letting his horse go, Lord Beaupré broke off, while Bolton-Brown stood looking after him and saying to himself that perhaps he *didn't* know! The chapter of English oddities was long.

But on the morrow the announcement was in *The Morning Post*, and that surely made it authentic. It was doubtless only superficially singular that Guy Firminger should have found himself unable to achieve a call in Chester Street until this journal had been for several hours in circulation. He appeared there just before luncheon, and the first person who received him was Mrs. Gosselin. He had always liked her, finding her infallible on the question of behavior; but he was on this occasion more than ever struck with her ripe astuteness, her independent wisdom.

" I knew what you wanted, I knew what you needed, I knew the subject on which you had pressed her," the good lady said;

"and after Sunday I found myself really
haunted with your dangers. There was
danger in the air at Bosco, in your own
defended house ; it seemed to me too monstrous. I said to myself, 'We *can* help him,
poor dear, and we *must.* It's the least one
can do for so old and so good a friend.' I
decided what to do: I simply put this other
story about. In London that always answers. I knew that Mary pitied you really
as much as I do, and that what she saw at
Bosco had been a revelation—had at any
rate brought your situation home to her.
Yet, of course, she would be shy about saying out, for herself, ' Here I am —I'll do
what you want.' The thing was for me to
say it *for* her ; so I said it first to that chat-
tering American. He repeated it to several
others, and there you are ! I just forced
her hand a little, but it's all right. All she
has to do is not to contradict it. It won't
be any trouble, and you'll be comfortable.
That will be our reward !" smiled Mrs.
Gosselin.

"Yes, all she has to do is not to contradict it," Lord Beaupré replied, musing a

moment. "It *won't* be any trouble," he
added, "and I *hope* I shall be comfortable."
He thanked Mrs. Gosselin formally and
liberally, and expressed all his impatience
to assure Mary herself of his deep obligation to her; upon which his hostess promised to send her daughter to him on the
instant: she would go and call her, so that
they might be alone. Before Mrs. Gosselin
left him, however, she touched on one or
two points that had their little importance.
Guy Firminger had asked for Hugh, but
Hugh had gone to the City, and his mother
mentioned candidly that he didn't take
part in the game. She even disclosed his
reason: he thought there was a want of
dignity in it. Lord Beaupré stared at this,
and after a moment exclaimed: "Dignity?
Dignity be hanged! One must save one's
life!"

"Yes, but the point poor Hugh makes is
that one must save it by the use of one's
own wits, or one's *own* arms and legs. But
do you know what I said to him?" Mrs.
Gosselin continued.

"Something very clever, I dare say."

"That if *we* were drowning, you'd be the
very first to jump in.   And we may fall
overboard yet!"   Fidgeting there, with his
hands in his pockets, Lord Beaupré gave a
laugh at this, but assured her that there
was nothing in the world for which they
mightn't count upon him.   None the less
she just permitted herself another warning,
a warning, it is true, that was in his own
interest, a reminder of a peril that he ought
beforehand to look in the face.   Wasn't
there always the chance — just the bare
chance — that a girl in Mary's position
would, in the event, decline to let him off,
decline to release him even on the day he
should wish to marry?   She wasn't speaking of Mary, but there were, of course, girls
who would play him that trick.   Guy Firminger considered this contingency ; then he
declared that it wasn't a question of "girls,"
it was simply a question of dear old Mary !
If *she* should wish to hold him, so much the
better ; he would do anything in the world
that she wanted.   "Don't let us dwell on
such vulgarities ; but I had it on my conscience!" Mrs. Gosselin wound up.

She left him, but at the end of three minutes Mary came in, and the first thing she said was: "Before you speak a word, please understand this, that it's wholly mamma's doing. I hadn't dreamed of it, but she suddenly began to tell people."

"It was charming of her, and it's charming of you!" the visitor cried.

"It's not charming of any one, I think," said Mary Gosselin, looking at the carpet. "It's simply idiotic."

"Don't be nasty about it. It will be tremendous fun."

"I've only consented because mamma says we owe it to you," the girl went on.

"Never mind your reason—the end justifies the means. I can never thank you enough, nor tell you what a weight it lifts off my shoulders. Do you know I feel the difference already?—a peace that passeth understanding!" Mary replied that this was childish; how could such a feeble fiction last? At the very best it could live but an hour, and then he would be no better off than before. It would bristle, moreover, with difficulties and absurdities;

it would be so much more trouble than it
was worth. She reminded him that so
ridiculous a service had never been asked
of any girl, and at this he seemed a little
struck; he said: "Ah, well, if it's positively
disagreeable to you, we'll instantly drop the
idea. But I — I thought you really liked
me enough—" She turned away impatient-
ly, and he went on to argue imperturbably
that she had always treated him in the
kindest way in the world. He added that
the worst was over—the start—they were
off; the thing would be in all the evening
papers. Wasn't it much simpler to accept
it? That was all they would have to do;
and all *she* would have to do would be not
to gainsay it, and to smile and thank people
when she was congratulated. She would
have to *act* a little, but that would just be
part of the fun. Oh, he hadn't the shadow
of a scruple about taking the world in; the
world deserved it richly, and she couldn't
deny that this was what she had felt for him,
that she had really been moved to compassion. He grew eloquent and charged
her with having recognized in his predica-

ment a genuine motive for charity. Their
little plot would last what it could — it
would be a part of their amusement to *make*
it last. Even if it should be but a thing of
a day, there would have been always so much
gained. But they would be ingenious, they
would find ways, they would have no end of
sport.

"*You* must be ingenious; I can't," said
Mary. "If people scarcely ever see us together, they'll guess we're trying to humbug
them."

"But they *will* see us together. We *are*
together. We've been together — I mean
we've seen a lot of each other — all our
lives."

"Ah, not *that* way!"

"Oh, trust me to work it right!" cried
the young man, whose imagination had now
evidently begun to glow in the air of their
pious fraud.

"You'll find it a dreadful bore," said
Mary Gosselin.

"Then I'll drop it, don't you see? And
you'll drop it, of course, the moment *you*'ve
had enough," Lord Beaupré punctually

added. " But as soon as you begin to
realize what a lot of good you do me you
won't *want* to drop it. That is, if you're
what I take you for!" laughed his lordship.

If a third person had been present at
this conversation — and there was nothing
in it surely that might not have been spoken
before a trusty listener—that person would
perhaps have thought, from the immediate
expression of Mary Gosselin's face, that
she was on the point of exclaiming, " You
take me for too big a fool!" No such un-
gracious words in fact, however, passed her
lips; she only said, after an instant, "What
reason do you propose to give, on the day
you need one, for our rupture?"

Her interlocutor stared. " To you, do
you mean?"

"*I* sha'n't ask you for one. I mean to
other people."

" Oh, I'll tell them you're sick of me.
I'll put everything on you, and you'll put
everything on me."

"You *have* worked it out!" Mary exclaimed.

"Oh, I shall be intensely considerate."

"Do you call that being considerate — publicly accusing me?"

Guy Firminger stared again. "Why, isn't that the reason *you*'ll give?"

She looked at him an instant. "I won't tell you the reason I shall give."

"Oh, I shall learn it from others."

"I hope you'll like it when you do!" said Mary, with sudden gayety; and she added frankly though kindly, the hope that he might soon light upon some young person who would really meet his requirements. He replied that he shouldn't be in a hurry — that was now just the comfort; and she, as if thinking over to the end the list of arguments against his clumsy contrivance, broke out, "And of course you mustn't dream of giving me anything — any tokens or presents."

"Then it won't look natural."

"That's exactly what I say. You can't make it deceive anybody."

"I *must* give you something—something that people can see. There must be some evidence! You can simply put my offer-

ings away after a little and give them back."
But about this Mary was visibly serious;
she declared that she wouldn't touch anything that came from his hand, and she
spoke in such a tone that he colored a
little and hastened to say, "Oh, all right,
I shall be thoroughly careful!" This appeared to complete their understanding; so
that after it was settled that for the deluded
world they *were* engaged, there was obvi-
ously nothing for him to do but to go. He
therefore shook hands with her very grate-
fully and departed.

V

HE was able promptly to assure his accomplice that their little plot was working
to a charm; it already made such a difference for the better. Only a week had
elapsed, but he felt quite another man; his
life was no longer spent in springing to
arms, and he had ceased to sleep in his
boots. The ghost of his great fear was laid;
he could follow out his inclinations and at-

tend to his neglected affairs. The news
had been a bomb in the enemy's camp, and
there were plenty of blank faces to testify
to the confusion it had wrought. Every
one was "sold," and every one made haste
to clap him on the back. Lottie Firminger
only had written in terms of which no notice could be taken, though, of course, he
expected every time he came in to find her
waiting in his hall. Her mother was coming up to town, and he should have the family on his back; but taking them as a single
body he could manage them, and that was
a detail. The Ashburys had remained at
Bosco till that establishment was favored
with the tidings that so nearly concerned it
(they were communicated to Maud's mother
by the house-keeper), and then the beautiful
sufferer had found in her defeat strength to
seek another asylum. The two ladies had
departed for a destination unknown; he
didn't think they had turned up in London.
Guy Firminger averred that there were precious portable objects which he was sure he
should miss on returning to his country
home.

He came every day to Chester Street, and
was evidently much less bored than Mary
had prefigured by this regular tribute to
verisimilitude.   It was amusement enough
to see the progress of their comedy and to
invent new touches for some of its scenes.
The girl herself was amused; it was an opportunity like another for cleverness such
as hers, and had much in common with private theatricals, especially with the rehears-
als, the most amusing part.   Moreover, she
was good-natured enough to be really pleased
at the service it was impossible for her not
to acknowledge that she had rendered.   Each
of the parties to this queer contract had anecdotes and suggestions for the other, and
each reminded the other duly that they
must at every step keep their story straight.
Except for the exercise of this care Mary
Gosselin found her duties less onorous than
she had feared, and her part in general much
more passive than active.   It consisted, indeed, largely of murmuring thanks and smiling and looking happy and handsome; as
well as, perhaps, also in saying, in answer to
many questions, that nothing as yet was

fixed, and of trying to remain humble when people expressed without ceremony that such a match was a wonder for such a girl. Her mother, on the other hand, was devotedly active. She treated the situation with private humor but with public zeal, and, making it both real and ideal, told so many fibs about it that there were none left for Mary. The girl had failed to understand Mrs. Gosselin's interest in this elaborate pleasantry; the good lady had seen in it from the first more than she herself had been able to see. Mary performed her task mechanically, sceptically; but Mrs. Gosselin attacked hers with conviction, and had really the air at moments of thinking that their fable had crystallized into fact. Mary allowed her as little of this attitude as possible, and was ironical about her duplicity —warnings which the elder lady received with gayety, until one day when repetition had made them act on her nerves. Then she begged her daughter, with sudden asperity, not to talk to her as if she were a fool. She had already had words with Hugh about some aspects of the affair—so

much as this was evident in Chester Street—
a smothered discussion which at the moment had determined the poor boy to go to
Paris with Bolton-Brown. The young men
came back together after Mary had been
"engaged" three weeks, but she remained
in ignorance of what passed between Hugh
and his mother the night of his return. She
had gone to the opera with Lady Whiteroy,
after one of her invariable comments on
Mrs. Gosselin's invariable remark that of
course Guy Firminger would spend his
evening in their box. The remedy for his
trouble, Lord Beaupré's prospective bride
had said, was surely worse than the disease ;
she was in perfect good faith when she
wondered that his lordship's sacrifices, his
laborious cultivation of appearances should
" pay."

Hugh Gosselin dined with his mother,
and at dinner talked of Paris and of what
he had seen and done there ; he kept the
conversation superficial, and after he had
heard how his sister, at the moment, was
occupied, asked no question that might have
seemed to denote an interest in the success

of the experiment for which in going abroad he had declined responsibility. His mother could not help observing that he never mentioned Guy Firminger by either of his names, and it struck her as a part of the same detachment that later, up-stairs (she sat with him while he smoked), he should suddenly say, as he finished a cigar :

" I return to New York next week."

" Before your time? What for?" Mrs. Gosselin was horrified.

" Oh, mamma, you know what for !"

" Because you still resent poor Mary's good-nature?"

" I don't understand it, and I don't like things I don't understand; therefore I'd rather not be here to see it. Besides, I really can't tell a pack of lies."

Mrs. Gosselin exclaimed and protested; she had arguments to prove that there was no call at present for the least deflection from the truth ; all that any one had to reply to any question (and there could be none that was embarrassing save the ostensible determination of the date of the marriage) was that nothing was settled as yet—

a form of words in which for the life of her
she couldn't see any perjury. " Why, then,
go in for anything in such bad taste, to
culminate only in something so absurd ?"
Hugh demanded. " If the essential part of
the matter can't be spoken of as fixed nothing is fixed, the deception becomes transparent, and they give the whole idea away.
It's child's play."

" That's why it's so innocent. All I can
tell you is that practically their attitude
answers ; he's delighted with its success.
Those dreadful women have given him up ;
they've already found some other victim."

" And how is it all to end, please ?"

Mrs. Gosselin was silent a moment.
" Perhaps it won't end."

" Do you mean that the engagement will
become real ?"

Again the good lady said nothing until
she broke out : " My dear boy, can't you
trust your poor old mummy ?"

" Is *that* your speculation ? Is that Mary's ? I never heard of anything so odious !" Hugh Gosselin cried. But she defended his sister with eagerness, with a

gloss of coaxing, maternal indignation, declaring that Mary's disinterestedness was complete—she had the perfect proof of it. Hugh was conscious, as he lighted another cigar, that the conversation was more fundamental than any that he had ever had with his mother, who, however, hung fire but for an instant when he asked her what this "perfect proof" might be. He didn't doubt of his sister, he admitted that; but the perfect proof would make the whole thing more luminous. It took finally the form of a confession from Mrs. Gosselin that the girl evidently liked — well, greatly liked — Mr. Bolton-Brown. Yes, the good lady had seen for herself at Bosco that the smooth young American was making up to her, and that, time and opportunity aiding, something might very well happen which could not be regarded as satisfactory. She had been very frank with Mary, had besought her not to commit herself to a suitor who in the very nature of the case couldn't meet the most legitimate of their views. Mary, who pretended not to know what their "views" were, had denied that she was in danger; but Mrs. Gosselin had assured her that she had all the air of it, and had said, triumphantly, "Agree to what Lord Beaupré asks of you, and I'll *believe* you." Mary had wished to be believed—so she had agreed. That was all the witchcraft any one had used.

Mrs. Gosselin out-talked her son, but there were two or three plain questions that he came back to; and the first of these bore upon the ground of her aversion to poor Bolton-Brown. He told her again, as he had told her before, that his friend was that rare bird, a maker of money who was also a man of culture. He was a gentleman to his finger-tips, accomplished, capable, kind, with a charming mother and two lovely sisters (she should see them !), the sort of fellow, in short, whom it was stupid not to appreciate.

"I believe it all; and if I had three daughters he should be very welcome to one of them."

"You might easily have had three daughters who wouldn't attract him at all ! You've had the good-fortune to have one who does, and I think you do wrong to interfere with it."

"My eggs are in one basket then, and that's a reason the more for preferring Lord Beaupré," said Mrs. Gosselin.

"Then it *is* your calculation — " stammered Hugh, in dismay; on which she colored and requested that he would be a little less rough with his mother. She would rather part with him immediately, sad as that would be, than that he should attempt to undo what she had done. When Hugh replied that it was not to Mary but to Beaupré himself that he judged it important he should speak, she informed him that a rash remonstrance might do his sister a cruel wrong. Dear Guy was *most* attentive.

" If you mean that he really cares for her there's the less excuse for his taking such a liberty with her. He's either in love with her or he isn't. If he is, let him make her a serious offer; if he isn't, let him leave her alone."

Mrs. Gosselin looked at her son with a kind of patient joy. " He's in love with her, but he doesn't know it."

"He ought to know it; and if he's so idiotic, I don't see that we ought to consider him."

"Don't worry—he *shall* know it!" Mrs. Gosselin cried; and, continuing to struggle with Hugh, she insisted on the delicacy of the situation. She made a certain impression on him, though on confused grounds; she spoke at one moment as if he was to forbear because the matter was a make-believe that happened to contain a convenience for a distressed friend, and at another as if one ought to strain a point because there were great possibilities at stake. She was most lucid when she pictured the social position and other advantages of a peer of the realm. What had those of an American stock-broker, however amiable and with whatever shrill belongings in the background, to compare with them? She was inconsistent, but she was diplomatic, and the result of the discussion was that Hugh Gosselin became conscious of a dread of "injuring" his sister. He became conscious at the same time of a still greater apprehension, that of seeing her arrive at the agreeable in a tortuous, a second-rate manner. He might keep the peace to please his mother, but he couldn't enjoy it, and he actually took his departure, travelling in company with Bolton-Brown, who, of course, before going waited on the ladies in Chester Street to thank them for the kindness they had shown him. It couldn't be kept from Guy Firminger that Hugh was not happy, though when they met, which was only once or twice before he quitted London, Mary Gosselin's brother flattered himself that he was too proud to show it. He had always liked old loafing Guy, and it was disagreeable to him not to like him now; but he was aware that he must either quarrel with him definitely or not at all, and that he had passed his word to his mother. Therefore his attitude was strictly negative; he took with the parties to it no notice whatever of the "engagement," and he couldn't help it if to other people he had the air of not being initiated. They doubtless thought him strangely fastidious. Perhaps he was; the tone of London struck him in some respects as very horrid; he had grown in a manner away from it. Mary was impenetrable; tender, gay, charming, but with no patience, as she said, for his premature flight. Except when Lord Beau-pré was present, you would not have dreamed that he existed for her. In his company — he had to be present more or less of course—she was simply like any other English girl who disliked effusiveness. They had each the same manner, that of persons of rather a shy tradition who were on their guard against public "spooning." They practised their fraud with good taste, a good taste mystifying to Bolton-Brown, who thought their precautions excessive. When he took leave of Mary Gosselin her eyes consented for a moment to look deep down into his. He had been from the first of the opinion that they were beautiful, and he was more mystified than ever.

If Guy Firminger had failed to ask Hugh Gosselin whether he had a fault to find with what they were doing, this was, in spite of old friendship, simply because he was too happy now to care much whom he didn't please, to care, at any rate, for criticism. He

had ceased to be critical himself, and his
high prosperity could take his blameless-
ness for granted. His happiness would
have been offensive if people generally
hadn't liked him, for it consisted of a kind
of monstrous candid comfort. To take all
sorts of things for granted was still his
great, his delightful characteristic; but it
didn't prevent his showing imagination and
tact and taste in particular circumstances.
He made, in their little comedy, all the
right jokes and none of the wrong ones;
the girl had an acute sense that there were
some jokes that would have been detestable. She gathered that it was univer-
sally supposed she was having an unprece-
dented season, and something of the glory
of an enviable future seemed indeed to
hang about her. People no doubt thought
it odd that she didn't go about more with
her future husband; but those who knew
anything about her knew that she had never
done exactly as other girls did. She had
her own ways, her own freedoms, and her
own scruples. Certainly he made the London weeks much richer than they had ever

been for a subordinate young person; he
put more things into them, so that they grew
dense and complicated. This frightened her
at moments, especially when she thought
with compunction that she was deceiving
her very friends. She didn't mind taking
the vulgar world in, but there were people
she hated not to enlighten, to reassure.
She could undeceive no one now, and, indeed, she would have been ashamed. There
were hours when she wanted to stop — she
had such a dread of doing too much; hours
when she thought with dismay that the
fiction of the rupture was still to come, with
its horrid train of new untrue things. She
spoke of it repeatedly to her confederate,
who only postponed and postponed, told
her she would never dream of forsaking
him if she measured the good she was
doing him. She did measure it, however,
when she met him in the great world; she
was of course always meeting him; that
was the only way appearances were kept
up. There was a certain attitude she could
allow him to take on these occasions; it
covered and carried off their subterfuge.

He could talk to her unmolested; for herself she never spoke of anything but the charming girls, everywhere present, among whom he could freely choose. He didn't protest, because to choose freely was what he wanted, and they discussed these young ladies one by one. Some she recommended, some she disparaged, but it was almost the only subject she tolerated. It was her system, in short, and she wondered he didn't get tired of it; she was so tired of it herself.

She tried other things that she thought he might find wearisome, but his good-humor was magnificent. He was now really for the first time enjoying his promotion, his wealth, his insight into the terms on which the world offered itself to the happy few, and these terms made a mixture healing to irritation. Once, at some glittering ball, he asked her if she should be jealous if he were to dance again with Lady Whiteroy, with whom he had danced already, and this was the only occasion on which he had come near making a joke of the wrong sort. She showed him what she thought of it and

made him feel that the way to be forgiven
was to spend the rest of the evening with
that lovely creature. Now that the phalanx
of the pressingly nubile was held in check
there was accordingly nothing to prevent his
passing his time pleasantly. Before he had
taken this effective way the diplomatic
mother, when she spied him flirting with a
married woman, felt that in urging a virgin
daughter's superior claims she worked for
righteousness as well as for the poor girl.
But Mary Gosselin protected these scandals
practically by the still greater scandal of her
indifference; so that he was in the odd
position of having waited to be confined to
know what it was to be at large. He had,
in other words, the maximum of security
with the minimum of privation. The lovely
creatures of Lady Whiteroy's order thought
Mary Gosselin charming, but they were the
first to see through her falsity.

All this carried our precious pair to the
middle of July; but nearly a month before
that, one night under the summer stars, on
the deck of the steamer that was to reach
New York on the morrow, something had

passed between Hugh Gosselin and his
brooding American friend. The night was
warm and splendid; these were their last
hours at sea, and Hugh, who had been
playing whist in the cabin, came up very
late to take an observation before turning
in. It was in this way that he chanced on
his companion, who was leaning over the
stern of the ship and gazing off, beyond its
phosphorescent track, at the muffled, moan-
ing ocean, the backward darkness, everything he had relinquished. Hugh stood by
him for a moment and then asked him
what he was thinking about. Bolton-Brown
gave at first no answer; after which he
turned round and, with his back against
the guard of the deck, looked up at the
multiplied stars. "He has it badly,"
Hugh Gosselin mentally commented. At
last his friend replied: "About something
you said yesterday."

"I forget what I said yesterday."

"You spoke of your sister's intended
marriage; it was the only time you had
spoken of it. You seemed to intimate that
it might not after all take place."

Hugh hesitated a little. "Well, it *won't* take place. They're not engaged, not really. This is a secret, a preposterous secret. I wouldn't tell any one else, but I'm willing to tell *you*. It may make a difference to you."

Bolton-Brown turned his head; he looked at Hugh a minute through the fresh darkness. "It does make a difference to me. But I don't understand," he added.

"Neither do I. I don't like it. It's a pretence, a temporary make-believe, to help Beaupré through."

"Through what?"

"He's so run after."

The young American stared, ejaculated, mused. "Oh, yes—your mother told me."

"It's a sort of invention of my mother's and a notion of his own (very absurd, I think), till he can see his way. Mary serves as a kind of escort for these first exposed months. It's ridiculous, but I don't know that it hurts her."

"Oh!" said Bolton-Brown.

"I don't know either that it does her any good."

"No!" said Bolton - Brown. Then he added: "It's certainly very kind of her."

"It's a case of old friends," Hugh explained, inadequately as he felt. "He has always been in and out of our house."

"But how will it end?"

"I haven't the least idea."

Bolton-Brown was silent; he faced about to the stern again and stared at the rush of the ship. Then shifting his position once more: "Won't the engagement, before they've done, develop into the regular thing?"

Hugh felt as if his mother were listening. "I dare say not. If there were even a remote chance of that, Mary wouldn't have consented."

"But mayn't *he* easily find that—charming as she is—he's in love with her?"

"He's too much taken up with himself."

"That's just a reason," said Bolton-Brown. "Love is selfish." He considered a moment longer, then he went on: "And mayn't *she* find—"

"Find what?" said Hugh, as he hesitated.

"Why, that she likes him."

"She likes him, of course, else she wouldn't have come to his assistance. But her certainty about herself must have been just what made her not object to lending herself to the arrangement. She could do it decently because she doesn't seriously care for him. If she did—" Hugh suddenly stopped.

"If she did?" his friend repeated.

"It would have been odious."

"I see," said Bolton-Brown, gently. "But how will they break off?"

"It will be Mary who'll break off."

"Perhaps she'll find it difficult."

"She'll require a pretext."

"I see," mused Bolton-Brown, shifting his position again.

"She'll find one," Hugh declared.

"I hope so," his companion responded.

For some minutes neither of them spoke; then Hugh asked: "Are you in love with her?"

"Oh, my dear fellow!" Bolton-Brown wailed. He instantly added, "Will it be any use for me to go back?"

Again Hugh felt as if his mother were listening; but he answered, "*Do* go back."

"It's awfully strange," said Bolton-Brown. "I'll go back."

"You had better wait a couple of months, you know."

"Mayn't I lose her then?"

"No; they'll drop it all."

"I'll go back," the American repeated, as if he hadn't heard. He was restless, agitated; he had evidently been much affected. He fidgeted away dimly, moved up the level length of the deck. Hugh Gosselin lingered longer at the stern; he fell into the attitude in which he had found the other, leaning over it and looking back at the great vague distance they had come. He thought of his mother.

VI

To remind her fond parent of the vanity of certain expectations which she more than suspected her of entertaining, Mary Gosselin, while she felt herself intensely watched (it had all brought about a horrid new situation at home), produced every day some fresh illustration of the fact that people were no longer imposed upon. Moreover, these illustrations were not invented; the girl believed in them, and when once she had begun to note them she saw them multiply fast. Lady Whiteroy, for one, was distinctly suspicious; she had taken the liberty more than once of asking the future Lady Beaupré what in the world was the matter with her. Brilliant figure as she was, and occupied with her own pleasures, which were of a very independent nature, she had, nevertheless, constituted herself Miss Gosselin's social sponsor: she took a particular interest in her marriage—an interest all the greater as it rested not only on a freely-professed regard for her, but on a keen sympathy with the other party to the transaction. Lady Whiteroy, who was very pretty and very clever, and whom Mary secretly but profoundly mistrusted, delighted in them both, in short; so much so, that Mary judged herself happy to be in a false position, so certain should she have been to be

jealous had she been in a true one. This
charming woman threw out inquiries that
made the girl not care to meet her eyes;
and Mary ended by forming a theory of the
sort of marriage for Lord Beaupré that Lady
Whiteroy really would have appreciated. It
would have been a marriage to a fool, a
marriage to Maud Ashbury or to Charlotte
Firminger. She would have her reasons for
preferring that; and as regarded the actual
prospect, she had only discovered that Mary
was even more astute than herself.

It will be understood how much our
young lady was on the crest of the wave,
when I mention that in spite of this complicated consciousness she was one of the ornaments (Guy Firminger was of course another) of the party entertained by her zealous
friend and Lord Whiteroy during the Good-
wood week. She came back to town with
the firm intention of putting an end to a
comedy which had more than ever become
odious to her; in consequence of which she
had on this subject with her fellow-comedian
a scene—the scene she had dreaded—half
pathetic half ridiculous. He appealed to

her, wrestled with her, took his usual ground
that she was saving his life without really
lifting a finger. He denied that the public
was not satisfied with their pretexts for
postponement, their explanations of delay;
what else was expected of a man who would
wish to celebrate his nuptials on a suitable
scale, but who had the misfortune to have
had, one after another, three grievous be-
reavements? He promised not to molest
her for the next three months, to go away
till his "mourning" was over, to go abroad,
to let her do as she liked. He wouldn't
come near her, he wouldn't even write (no
one would know it), if she would let him
keep up the mere form of their fiction; and
he would let her off the very first instant he
definitely perceived that this expedient had
ceased to be effective. She couldn't judge
of that—she must let *him* judge; and it was
a matter in which she could surely trust to
his honor.

Mary Gosselin trusted to it, but she insisted on his going away. When he took
such a tone as that she couldn't help being
moved; he breathed with such frank, gen-

erous lips on the irritation she had stored
up against him.   Guy Firminger went to
Homburg; and if his confederate consented not to clip the slender thread by which
this particular engagement still hung, she
made very short work with every other.   A
dozen invitations, for Cowes, for the country, for Scotland, shimmered there before
her, made a pathway of flowers, but she
sent barbarous excuses.   When her mother,
aghast, said to her, "What, then, will you
do?" she replied, in a very conclusive manner, "I'll go home!"   Mrs. Gosselin was
wise enough not to struggle; she saw that
the thread was delicate, that it must dangle
in quiet air.   She therefore travelled back
with her daughter to homely Hampshire,
feeling that they were people of less importance than they had been for many a
week.   On the August afternoons they sat
again on the little lawn on which Guy Firminger had found them the day he first became eloquent about the perils of the de-
sirable young bachelor; and it was on this
very spot that, towards the end of the month,
and with some surprise, they beheld Mr.

Bolton - Brown once more approach. He
had come back from America; he had arrived but a few days before; he was staying, of all places in the world, at the inn in
the village.

His explanation of this caprice was of all
explanations the oddest: he had come three
thousand miles for the love of water-colors.
There was nothing more sketchable than
the sketchability of Hampshire—wasn't it
celebrated, classic? and he was so good as
to include Mrs. Gosselin's charming prem-
ises, and even their charming occupants, in
his view of the field. He fell to work with
speed, with a sort of feverish eagerness; he
seemed possessed, indeed, by the frenzy of
the brush. He sketched everything on the
place, and when he had represented an object once he went straight at it again. His
advent was soothing to Mary Gosselin, in
spite of his nervous activity; it must be admitted, indeed, that at the moment he arrived she had already felt herself in quieter
waters. The August afternoons, the relin-
quishment of London, the simplified life,
had rendered her a service which, if she had

freely qualified it, she would have described as a restoration of her self-respect. If poor Guy found any profit in such conditions as these, there was no great reason to repudiate him. She had so completely shaken off responsibility that she took scarcely more than a languid interest in the fact, communicated to her by Lady Whiteroy, that Charlotte Firminger had also, as the newspapers said, "proceeded" to Homburg. Lady Whiteroy knew, for Lady Whiteroy had "proceeded" as well; her physician had discovered in her constitution a pressing need for the comfort imbibed in dripping matutinal tumblers. She chronicled Charlotte's presence, and even to some extent her behavior, among the haunters of the spring, but it was not till some time afterwards that Mary learned how Miss Firminger's pilgrimage had been made under her ladyship's protection. This was a further sign that, like Mrs. Gosselin, Lady Whiteroy had ceased to struggle; she had, in town, only shrugged her shoulders ambiguously on being informed that Lord Beaupré's intended was going down to her stupid home.

The fulness of Mrs. Gosselin's renunciation was apparent during the stay of the
young American in the neighborhood of
that retreat. She occupied herself with her
knitting, her garden, and the cares of a punc-
tilious hospitality, but she had no appearance of any other occupation. When people came to tea Bolton-Brown was always
there, and she had the self-control to attempt
to say nothing that could assuage their natural surprise. Mrs. Ashbury came one day
with poor Maud, and the two elder ladies,
as they had done more than once before,
looked for some moments into each other's
eyes. This time it was not a look of defi-
ance; it was rather—or it would have been
for an observer completely in the secret—a
look of reciprocity, of fraternity, a look of
arrangement. There was, however, no one
completely in the secret save perhaps Mary,
and Mary didn't heed. The arrangement,
at any rate, was ineffectual; Mrs. Gosselin
might mutely say, over the young American's eager, talkative shoulders, "Yes, you
may have him if you can get him:" the
most rudimentary experiments demonstrat-

ed that he was not to be got.   Nothing
passed on this subject between Mary and
her mother, whom the girl none the less
knew to be holding her breath and continuing to watch.   She counted it more and
more as one unpleasant result of her con-
spiracy with Guy Firminger, that it almost
poisoned a relation that had always been
sweet.   It was to show that she was independent of it that she did as she liked now,
which was almost always as Bolton-Brown
liked.   When in the first days of Septem-
ber—it was in the warm, clear twilight, and
they happened, amid the scent of fresh hay,
to be leaning side by side on a stile—he
gave her a view of the fundamental and
esoteric, as distinguished from the convenient and superficial motive of his having
come back to England, she of course made
no allusion to a prior tie.   On the other
hand, she insisted on his going up to London by the first train the next day.   He was
to wait—that was distinctly understood—
for his satisfaction.

She desired, meanwhile, to write immediately to Guy Firminger, but as he had kept

his promise of not complicating their contract with letters she was uncertain as to his
actual whereabouts ; she was only sure he
would have left Homburg. Lady Whiteroy had become silent, so there were no
more side-lights, and she was on the point
of telegraphing to London for an address
when she received a telegram from Bosco.
The proprietor of that seat had arrived there
the day before, and he found he could make
trains fit if she would on the morrow allow him to come over and see her for a
day or two. He had returned sooner than
their agreement allowed, but she answered,
"Come," and she showed his missive to
her mother, who at the sight of it wept
with strange passion. Mary said to her,
" For Heaven's sake, don't let him see
you !" She lost no time : she told him on
the morrow, as soon as he entered the
house, that she couldn't keep it up another
hour.

"All right—it *is* no use," he conceded ;
" they're at it again !"

" You see you've gained nothing," she replied, triumphantly. She had instantly rec-

ognized that he was different, how much had happened.

"I've gained some of the happiest days of my life."

"Oh, that was not what you tried for!"

"Indeed it was, and I got exactly what I wanted," said Guy Firminger. They were in the cool little drawing-room where the morning light was dim. Guy Firminger had a sunburnt appearance, as in England people returning from other countries are apt to have, and Mary thought he had never looked so well. It was odd, but it was noticeable, that he had grown much handsomer since he had become a personage. He paused a moment, smiling at her while her mysterious eyes rested on him, and then he added: "Nothing ever worked better. It's no use now—people see. But I've got a start. I wanted to turn round and look about, and I *have* turned round and looked about. There are things I've escaped. I'm afraid you'll never understand how deeply I'm indebted to you."

"Oh, it's all right," said Mary Gosselin.

There was another short silence, after

which he went on : " I've come back sooner
than I promised, but only to be strictly fair.
I began to see that we couldn't hold out,
and that it was my duty to let you off.
From that moment I was bound to put an
end to your situation. I might have done
so by letter, but that seemed scarcely de-
cent. It's all I came back for, you know,
and it's why I wired to you yesterday."

Mary hesitated an instant; she reflected
intensely. What had happened, what would
happen, was that if she didn't take care the
signal for the end of their little arrangement
would not have appeared to come from herself. She particularly wished it not to
come from any one else, she had even a horror of that ; so that after an instant she
hastened to say, "I was on the very point
of wiring to *you*—I was only waiting for
your address."

" Wiring to me?" He seemed rather
blank.

" To tell you that our absurd affair really,
this time, can't go on another day—to put
a complete stop to it."

" Oh !" said Guy Firminger.

" So it's all right."

" You've always hated it !" Guy laughed;
and his laugh sounded slightly foolish to
the girl.

" I found yesterday that I hated it more
than ever."

Lord Beaupré showed a quickened attention. " For what reason—yesterday ?"

" I would rather not tell you, please. Perhaps some time you'll find it out."

He continued to look at her brightly and
fixedly, with his confused cheerfulness.
Then he said, with a vague, courteous alac-
rity, " I see, I see !" She had an impression that he didn't see ; but it didn't matter,
she was nervous and quite preferred that he
shouldn't. They both got up, and in a moment he exclaimed : " Well, I'm intensely
sorry it's over ! It has been so charming."

" You've been very good about it; I mean
very reasonable," Mary said, to say something. Then she felt in her nervousness
that this was just what she ought not to
have said ; it sounded ironical and provok-
ing, whereas she had meant it as pure good-
nature. " Of course you'll stay to lunch-

eon?" she continued. She was bound in
common hospitality to speak of that, and he
answered that it would give him the greatest pleasure. After this her apprehension
increased, and it was confirmed in particular by the manner in which he suddenly
asked:

"By-the-way, what reason shall we give?"

"What reason?"

"For our rupture. Don't let us seem to
have quarrelled."

"We can't help that," said Mary. "Nothing else will account for our behavior."

"Well, I sha'n't say anything about *you*."

"Do you mean you'll let people think it
was yourself who were tired of it?"

"I mean I sha'n't *blame* you."

"You ought to behave as if you cared!"
said Mary.

Guy Firminger laughed, but he looked
worried, and he evidently was puzzled.
"You must act as if you had jilted me."

"You're not the sort of person, unfortu-
nately, that people jilt."

Lord Beaupré appeared to accept this
statement as incontestable; not with ela-

tion, however, but with candid regret, the slightly embarrassed recognition of a fundamental obstacle. "Well, it's no one's business, at any rate, is it?"

"No one's, and that's what I shall say if people question me. Besides," Mary added, "they'll see for themselves."

"What will they see?"

"I mean they'll understand. And now we had better join mamma."

It was his evident inclination to linger in the room after he had said this that gave her complete alarm. Mrs. Gosselin was in another room, in which she sat in the morning, and Mary moved in that direction, pausing only in the hall for him to accompany her. She wished to get him into the presence of a third person. In the hall he joined her, and in doing so laid his hand gently on her arm. Then looking into her eyes with all the pleasantness of his honesty, he said: "It will be very easy for me to appear to care—for I *shall* care. I shall care immensely!" Lord Beaupré added, smiling.

Anything, it struck her, was better than that

—than that he should say: "We'll keep on, if you like, (*I* should !) only this time it will be serious. Hold me to it—do; don't let me go; lead me on to the altar, really!" Some such words as these, she believed, were rising to his lips, and she had an insurmountable horror of hearing them. It was as if, well enough meant on *his* part, they would do her a sort of dishonor, so that all her impulse was quickly to avert them. That was not the way she wanted to be asked in marriage. "Thank you very much," she said, " but it doesn't in the least matter. You will seem to have been jilted —so it's all right!"

"All right! You mean—" He hesitated, he had colored a little; his eyes questioned her.

" I'm engaged to be married—in earnest."

"Oh!" said Lord Beaupré.

"You asked me just now if I had a special reason for having been on the point of telegraphing to you, and I said I had. That was my special reason."

"I see!" said Lord Beaupré. He looked grave for a few seconds, then he gave an

awkward smile.   But he behaved with perfect tact and discretion, didn't even ask her
who the gentleman in the case might be.
He congratulated her in the dark, as it
were, and if the effect of this was indeed a
little odd, she liked him for his quick per-
ception of the fine fitness of pulling up
short.   Besides, he extracted the name of
the gentleman soon enough from her mother, in whose company they now immediately
found themselves.   Mary left Guy Firminger with the good lady for half an hour
before luncheon; and when the girl came
back it was to observe that she had been
crying again.   It was dreadful — what she
might have been saying.   Their guest, however, at luncheon was not lachrymose; he
was natural, but he was talkative and gay.
Mary liked the way he now behaved, and
more particularly the way he departed immediately after the meal.   As soon as he
was gone Mrs. Gosselin broke out, suppli-
antly: "Mary!"   But her daughter replied:

"I know, mamma, perfectly what you're
going to say, and if you attempt to say it I
shall leave the room."   With this threat

(day after day, for the following time) she kept the terrible appeal unuttered until it was too late for an appeal to be of use. That afternoon she wrote to Bolton-Brown that she accepted his offer of marriage.

Guy Firminger departed altogether; he went abroad again, and to far countries. He was therefore not able to be present at the nuptials of Miss Gosselin and the young American whom he had entertained at Bosco, which took place in the middle of November. Had he been in England, however, he probably would have felt impelled by a due regard for past verisimilitude to abstain from giving his countenance to such an occasion. His absence from the country contributed to the needed, even if astonishing, effect of his having been jilted; so, likewise, did the reputed vastness of Bolton-Brown's young income, which in London was grossly exaggerated. Hugh Gosselin had perhaps a little to do with this; as he had sacrificed a part of his summer holiday, he got another month and came out to his sister's wedding. He took public comfort in his brother-in-law; nevertheless he listened with attention to a curious communication made him by his mother after the young couple had started for Italy; even to the point of bringing out the inquiry (in answer to her assertion that poor Guy had been ready to place everything he had at Mary's feet) : " Then why the devil didn't he do it ?"

" From simple delicacy! He didn't want to make her feel as if she had lent herself to an artifice only on purpose to get hold of him—to treat her as if she, too, had been at bottom one of the very harpies she helped him to elude."

Hugh thought a moment. " That *was* delicate."

" He's the dearest creature in the world. He's on his guard, he's prudent, he tested himself by separation. Then he came back to England in love with her. She might have had it all!"

" I'm glad she didn't get it *that* way."

" She had only to wait—to put an end to their artifice, harmless as it was, for the present, but still wait. She might have broken off in a way that would have made it come on again better."

" That's exactly what she didn't want."

" I mean as a quite separate incident," said Mrs. Gosselin.

" *I* loathed their artifice, harmless as it was !" her son observed.

Mrs. Gosselin for a moment made no answer; then she turned away from the fire, into which she had been pensively gazing, with the ejaculation, " Poor dear Guy !"

" I can't for the life of me see that he's to be pitied."

" He'll marry Charlotte Firminger."

" If he's such an ass as that, it's his own affair."

" Bessie Whiteroy will bring it about."

" What has *she* to do with it ?"

" She wants to get hold of him."

" Then why will she marry him to another woman ?"

" Because in that way she can select the other—a woman he won't care for. It will keep him from taking some one that's nicer."

Hugh Gosselin stared—he laughed aloud. " Lord, mamma, you're deep !"

" Indeed I am. I see much more."

" What do you see ?"

"Mary won't in the least care for America. Don't tell me she will," Mrs. Gosselin added, "for you know perfectly you don't believe it."

"She'll care for her husband, she'll care . for everything that concerns him."

"He's very nice; in his little way he's delightful. But as an alternative to Lord Beaupré, he's ridiculous!"

"Mary's in a position in which she has nothing to do with alternatives."

"For the present, yes, but not forever. She'll have enough of your New York; they'll come back here. I see the future dark," Mrs. Gosselin pursued, inexorably musing.

"Tell me, then, all you see."

"She'll find poor Guy wretchedly married, and she'll be very sorry for him."

"Do you mean that he'll make love to her? You give a queer account of your paragon."

"He'll value her sympathy. I see life as it is."

"You give a queer account of your daughter."

"I don't give *any* account. She'll behave perfectly," Mrs. Gosselin somewhat inconsequently subjoined.

"Then what are you afraid of?"

"She'll be sorry for him, and it will be all a worry."

"A worry to whom?"

The good lady was silent a moment. "To me," she replied. "And to you as well."

"Then they mustn't come back."

"That will be a greater worry still."

"Surely not a greater—a smaller. We'll put up with the lesser evil."

"Nothing will prevent her coming to a sense, eventually, of what *might* have been. And when they *both* recognize it—"

"It will be very dreadful!" Hugh exclaimed, completing gayly his mother's phrase. "I don't see, however," he added, "what in all this you do with Bessie Whiteroy."

"Oh, he'll be tired of her; she's hard, she'll have become despotic. I see life as it is," the good lady repeated.

"Then all I can say is that it's not very

nice! But they sha'n't come back; *I*'ll attend to that!" said Hugh Gosselin, who has attended to it up to this time successfully, though the rest of his mother's prophecy is so far accomplished (it was her second hit) as that Charlotte Firminger is now, strange as it may seem, Lady Beaupré.

THE VISITS

THE other day, after her death, when they were discussing her, some one said, in reference to the great number of years she had lived, the people she had seen, and the stories she knew, "What a pity no one ever took any notes of her talk!" For a London epitaph that was almost exhaustive, and the subject presently changed. One of the listeners had taken many notes, but he didn't confess it on the spot. The following story is a specimen of my exactitude — I took it down *verbatim*, having that faculty, the day after I heard it. I choose it, at hazard, among those of her reminiscences that I have preserved; it's not worse than the others. I will give you some of the others too— when occasion offers—so that you may judge.

I met in town that year a dear woman whom I had scarcely seen since I was a girl ; she had dropped out of the world; she came up but once in five years. We had been together as very young creatures, and then we had married and gone our ways. It was arranged between us that after I should have paid a certain visit in August in the west of England I would take her — it would be very convenient, she was just over the Cornish border—on the way to my other engagements; I would work her in, as you say nowadays. She wanted immensely to show me her home, and she wanted still more to show me her girl, who had not come up to London, choosing instead, after much deliberation, to go abroad for a month with her brother and her brother's coach—he had been cramming for something—and Mrs. Coach of course. All that Mrs. Chantry had been able to show me in town was her husband, one of those country gentlemen with a moderate property and an old place, who are a part of the essence in their own neighborhood and not a part of anything anywhere else.

A couple of days before my visit to Chantry Court the people to whom I had

gone from town took me over to see some
friends of theirs, who lived ten miles away
in a place that was supposed to be fine.
As it was a long drive we stayed to luncheon; and then, as there were gardens and
other things that were more or less on show,
we struggled along to tea, so as to get home
just in time for dinner. There were a good
many other people present, and before
luncheon a very pretty girl came into the
drawing-room, a real maiden in her flower,
less than twenty, fresh and fair and charming, with the expression of some one I knew.
I asked who she was, and was told she was
Miss Chantry, so that in a moment I spoke
to her, mentioning that I was an old friend
of her mother's, and that I was coming to
pay them a visit. She looked rather frightened and blank, was apparently unable to
say that she had ever heard of me, and
hinted at no pleasure in the idea that she
was to hear of me again. But this didn't
prevent my perceiving that she was lovely,
for I was wise enough even then not to
think it necessary to measure people by the
impression that one makes on them. I saw

that any I should make on Louisa Chantry would be much too clumsy a test. She had been staying at the house at which I was calling; she had come alone, as the people were old friends and, to a certain extent, neighbors, and was going home in a few days. It was a daughterless house, but there was inevitable young life; a couple of girls from the vicarage, a married son and his wife, a young man who had "ridden over," and another young man who was staying.

Louisa Chantry sat opposite to me at luncheon, but too far for conversation, and before we got up I had discovered that if her manner to me had been odd, it was not because she was inanimate. She was, on the contrary, in a state of intense though carefully muffled vibration. There was some fever in her blood, but no one perceived it — no one, that is, with an exception — an exception which was just a part of the very circumstance. This single suspicion was lodged in the breast of the young man whom I have alluded to as staying in the house. He was on the same side of the table as myself and diagonally facing the girl; therefore what I learned about him was for the moment mainly what she told me; meaning by "she" her face, her eyes, her movements, her whole perverted personality. She was extremely on her guard, and I should never have guessed her secret but for an accident. The accident was that the only time she dropped her eyes upon him during the repast I happened to notice it. It might not have been much to notice, but it led to my seeing that there was a little drama going on, and that the young man would naturally be the hero. It was equally natural that in this capacity he should be the cause of my asking my left-hand neighbor, who happened to be my host, for some account of him. But "Oh, that fellow? he's my nephew," was a description which, to appear copious, required that I should know more about the uncle.

We had coffee on the terrace of the house; a terrace laid out in one quarter, oddly and charmingly, in grass, where the servants who waited upon us seemed to tread, processionally, on soundless velvet.

There I had a good look at my host's nephew and a longer talk with my friend's daughter, in regard to whom I had become conscious of a faint formless anxiety. I remember saying to her, gropingly, instinctively: "My dear child, can I do anything for you? I shall, perhaps, see your mother before you do. Can I, for instance, say anything to her *from* you?" This only made her blush and turn away; and it was not till too many days had passed that I guessed that what had looked out at me unwittingly in her little gazing trepidation was something like, "Oh, just take me away in spite of myself!" Superficially, conspicuously, there was nothing in the young man to take her away from. He was a person of the middle condition, and, save that he didn't look at all humble, might have passed for a poor relation. I mean that he had rather a seedy, shabby air, as if he were wearing out old clothes (he had on faded things that didn't match); and I formed vaguely the theory that he was a specimen of the numerous youthful class that goes to seek its fortune in the colonies, keeps

strange company there, and comes home
without a penny. He had a brown, smooth,
handsome face, a slightly swaggering, self-
conscious ease, and was probably objected
to in the house. He hung about, smoking
cigarettes on the terrace, and nobody seemed
to have much to say to him—a circumstance
which, as he managed somehow to convey,
left him absolutely indifferent. Louisa
Chantry strolled away with one of the girls
from the vicarage ; the party on the terrace
broke up, and the nephew disappeared.

It was settled that my friends and I
should take leave at half - past five, and
I begged to be abandoned in the interval
to my devices. I turned into the library
and, mounted on ladders, I handled old
books and old prints and soiled my gloves.
Most of the others had gone to look at the
church, and I was left in possession. I
wandered into the rooms in which I knew
there were pictures ; and if the pictures were
not good, there was some interesting china,
which I followed from corner to corner and
from cabinet to cabinet. At last I found
myself on the threshold of a small room

which appeared to terminate the series, and
in which, between the curtains draping the
doorways, there appeared to be rows of rare
old plates on velvet screens. I was on the
point of going in when I became aware that
there was something else besides, something
which threw me back. Two persons were
standing side by side at the window, looking
out together with their backs to me—two
persons as to whom I immediately felt that
they believed themselves to be alone and
unwatched. One of them was Louisa Chantry, the other was the young man whom
my host had described as his nephew.
They were so placed as not to see me, and
when I recognized them I checked myself
instinctively. I hesitated a moment; then
I turned away altogether. I can't tell you
why, except that if I had gone in I should
have had somehow the air of discovering
them. There was no visible reason why
they should have been embarrassed by discovery, inasmuch as, so far as I could see,
they were doing no harm, were only standing more or less together, without touching,
and for the moment apparently saying noth-

ing. Were they watching something out of
the window? I don't know; all I know is
that the observation I had made at luncheon gave me a sense of responsibility. I
might have taken my responsibility the other way and broken up their communion;
but I didn't feel this to be sufficiently my
business. Later on I wished I had.

I passed through the rooms again, and
then out of the house. The gardens were
ingenious, but they made me think (I have
always that conceited habit) how much
cleverer *I* should have been about them.
Presently I met several of the rest of the
party coming back from the church; on
which my hostess took possession of me,
declaring there was a point of view I must
absolutely be treated to. I saw she was a
walking woman, and that this meant half a
mile in the park. But I was good for that,
and we wandered off together while the
others returned to the house. It was present to me that I ought to ask my companion, for Helen Chantry's sake, a question
about Louisa — whether, for instance, she
had happened to notice the way the girl

seemed to be going.   But it was difficult to
say anything without saying too much; so
that, to begin with, I merely risked the observation that our young friend was remarkably pretty.   As the point admitted of no
discussion, this didn't take us very far; nor
was the subject much enlarged by our una-
nimity as to the fact that she was also
remarkably nice.   I observed that I had
had very little chance to talk with her, for
which I was sorry, having known her mother
for years. My hostess at this looked vaguely
round, as if she had missed her for the first
time. "Sure enough, she has not been
about. I dare say she's been writing to her
mother — she's always writing to her mother." "Not always," I mentally reflected; but
I waited discreetly, admiring everything and
rising to the occasion and the views, before
I inquired casually who the young man
might be who had sat two or three below
me at luncheon—the rather good-looking
young man, with the regular features and
the brownish clothes—not the one with the
mustache.

"Oh, poor Jack Brandon!" said my companion, in a tone calculated to make him seem no one in particular.

" Is he very poor ?" I asked, with a laugh.

"Oh, dear, yes. There are nine of them —fancy !—all boys ; and there's nothing for any one but the eldest. He's my husband's nephew—his poor mother's my sister-in-law. He sometimes turns up here when he has nothing better to do ; but I don't think he likes us much." I saw she meant that they didn't like *him;* and I exposed myself to suspicion by asking if he had been with them long; but my friend was not very plastic, and she simplified my whole theory of the case by replying, after she had thought a moment, that she wasn't clear about it—she thought he had come only the morning before. It seemed to me I could safely feel a little further, so I inquired if he were likely to stay many days. "Oh dear, no; he'll go to-morrow !" said my hostess. There was nothing whatever to show that she saw a connection between my odd interest in Mr. Brandon and the subject of our former reference ; there was only a quick lucidity on the subject of the young man's departure. It reassured me, for no great complications would have arisen in forty-eight hours.

In retracing our steps we passed again through a part of the gardens. Just after we had entered them my hostess, begging me to excuse her, called at a man who was raking leaves to ask him a question about his wife. I heard him reply, "Oh, she's very bad, my lady," and I followed my course. Presently my lady turned round with him, as if to go to see his wife, who apparently was ill and on the place. I continued to look about me — there were such charming things; and at the end of five minutes I missed my way—I had not taken the direction of the house. Suddenly at the turn of a walk, the angle of a great clipped hedge, I found myself face to face with Jack Brandon. He was moving rapidly, looking down, with his hands in his pockets, and he started and stared at me a moment. I said, "Oh, how d'ye do?" and I was on the point of adding, "Won't you kindly show me the right way?" But with a summary salute and a queer expression of face he had already passed me. I looked after him an instant and I all but stopped him; then one of the faintest voices of the air told me that Louisa Chantry would not be far off, that, in fact, if I were to go on a few steps I should find her. I continued, and I passed through an arched aperture of the hedge, a kind of door in the partition. This corner of the place was like an old French garden, a little enclosed apartment, with statues set into the niches of the high walls of verdure. I paused in admiration; then just opposite to me I saw poor Louisa. She was on a bench, with her hands clasped in her lap, her head bent, her eyes staring down before her. I advanced on the grass, attracting her attention; and I was close to her before she looked at me, before she sprang up and showed me a face convulsed with nameless pain. She was so pale that I thought she was ill — I had a vision of her companion's having rushed off for help. She stood gazing at me with expanded eyes and parted lips, and what I was mainly conscious of was that she had become ten years older. Whatever troubled her, it was something pitiful—

something that prompted me to hold out my two hands to her and exclaim, tenderly, "My poor child, my poor child!" She wavered a moment, as if she wanted to escape me but couldn't trust herself to run; she looked away from me, turning her head this way and that. Then, as I went close to her, she covered her face with her two hands, she let me lay mine upon her and draw her to my breast. As she dropped her head upon it she burst into tears, sobbing soundlessly and tragically. I asked her no question, I only held her so long as she would, letting her pour out the passion which I felt at the same time she made a tremendous effort to smother. She couldn't smother it, but she could break away violently; and this she quickly did, hurrying out of the nook where our little scene — and some other greater scene, I judged, just before it — had taken place, and leaving me infinitely mystified. I sat down on the bench a moment and thought it over; then I succeeded in discovering a path to the house.

The carriage was at the door for our drive home, but my companions, who had had tea, were waiting for our hostess, of whom they wished to take leave, and who had not yet come in. I reported her as engaged with the wife of one of the gardeners, but we lingered a little in the hall, a largeish group, to give her time to arrive. Two other persons were absent, one of whom was Louisa Chantry and the other the young man whom I had just seen quitting her in the garden. While I sat there, a trifle abstracted, still somewhat agitated by the sequel to that incident and at the same time impatient of our last vague dawdle, one of the footmen presented me with a little folded note. I turned away to open it, and at the very moment our hostess fortunately came in. This diverted the attention of the others from the action of the footman, whom, after I had looked at the note, I immediately followed into the drawing-room. He led me through it and through two or three others to the door of the little retreat in which, nearly an hour before, I had come upon Louisa Chantry and Mr. Brandon. The note was from Louisa; it contained the simple words: "Would you very kindly speak to me an instant before you go?" She was waiting for me in the most sequestered spot she had been able to select, and there the footman left us. The girl came straight at me and in an instant she had grasped my hands. I became aware that her condition had changed; her tears were gone, she had a concentrated purpose. I could scarcely see her beautiful young face — it was pressed, beseechingly, so close to mine. I only felt, as her dry, shining eyes almost dazzled me, that a strong light had been waved back and forth before me. Her words at first seemed to me incoherent; then I understood that she was asking me for a pledge.

"Excuse me, forgive me for bringing you here — to say something I can't say before all those people. *Do* forgive me—it was so awfully kind of you to come. I couldn't think of any other way — just for two seconds. I want you to swear to me," she went on, with her hands now raised and intensely clasped.

"To swear, dearest child?"

"I'm not your dearest child—I'm not

any one's! But *don't* tell mamma. Promise me—promise me," she insisted.

"Tell her what?—I don't understand."

"Oh, you do — you do!" she kept on; "and if you're going to Chantry you'll see her, you'll be with her, you may see her before I do. On my knees I ask you for a vow!"

She seemed on the point of throwing herself at my feet, but I stopped her. I kept her erect. "When shall *you* see your mother?"

"As soon as I can. I want to get home— I want to get home!" With this I thought she was going to cry again, but she controlled herself and only pressed me with feverish eyes.

"You have some great trouble. For Heaven's sake, tell me what it is."

"It isn't anything — it will pass. Only don't breathe it to mamma!"

"How can I breathe it if I don't know what it is?"

"You do know—you know what I mean." Then, after an instant's pause, she added: "What I did in the garden."

" *What* did you do in the garden ?"

"I threw myself on your neck and I sobbed
—I behaved like a maniac."

" Is that all you mean ?"

"It's what I don't want mamma to know—
it's what I beseech you to keep silent about.
If you don't, I'll never, never go home.
Have *mercy* on me !" the poor child qua-
vered.

" Dear girl, I only want to be tender to
you—to be perfect. But tell me first, has
any one acted wrongly to you ?"

" No one—*no* one. I speak the truth."

She looked into my eyes, and I looked
far into hers. They were wild with pain,
and yet they were so pure that they made
me confusedly believe her. I hesitated a
moment; then I risked the question : " Isn't
Mr. Brandon responsible for anything ?"

" For nothing—for nothing ! Don't blame
him !" the girl passionately cried.

" He hasn't made love to you !"

" Not a word—before God ! Oh, it was
too awful !" And with this she broke away
from me, flung herself on her knees before a
sofa, burying her face in it and in her arms.

"Promise me, promise me, promise me!" she continued to wail.

I was horribly puzzled, but I was immeasurably touched. I stood looking a moment at her extravagant prostration; then I said, "I'm dreadfully in the dark, but I promise."

This brought her to her feet again, and again she seized my hands. "Solemnly, sacredly?" she panted.

"Solemnly, sacredly."

"Not a syllable—not a hint?"

"Dear Louisa," I said, kindly, "when I promise I perform."

"You see I don't know you. And when do you go to Chantry?"

"Day after to-morrow. And when do you?"

"To-morrow, if I can."

"Then you'll see your mother first — it will be all right," I said, smiling.

"All right, all right!" she repeated, with her woful eyes. "Go, go!" she added, hearing a step in the adjoining room.

The footman had come back to announce that my friends were seated in the carriage, and I was careful to say before him in a different tone : " Then there's nothing more I can do for you ?"

" Nothing—good-bye," said Louisa, tearing herself away too abruptly to take my kiss, which, to follow the servant again, I left unbestowed. I felt awkward and guilty as I took leave of the company, murmuring something to my entertainers about having had an arrangement to make with Miss Chantry. Most of the people bade us good-bye from the steps, but I didn't see Jack Brandon. On our drive home in the waning afternoon my other friends doubtless found me silent and stupid.

I went to Chantry two days later, and was disappointed to find that the daughter of the house had not returned, though indeed after parting with her I had been definitely of the opinion that she was much more likely to go to bed and be ill. Her mother, however, had not heard that she was ill, and my inquiry about the young lady was of course full of circumspection. It was a little difficult, for I had to talk about her, Helen being particularly delighted that we had already made acquaintance. No day had been fixed for her return, but it came over my friend that she oughtn't to be absent during too much of my visit. She was the best thing they had to show—she was the flower and the charm of the place. It had other charms as well—it was a sleepy, silvery old home, exquisitely gray and exquisitely green; a house where you could have confidence in your leisure; it would be as genuine as the butter and the claret. The very look of the pleasant, prosaic drawing-room suggested long mornings of fancy work, of Berlin wool and premeditated patterns, new stitches and mild pauses. My good Helen was always in the middle of something eternal, of which the past and the future were rolled up in oil-cloth and tissue-paper, and the intensest moments of conversation were when it was spread out for pensive opinions. These used to drop sometimes even from Christopher Chantry when he straddled vaguely in with muddy leggings and the raw materials of a joke. He had a mind like a large, full milk-pan, and his wit was as thick as cream.

One evening I came down to dinner a little early and, to my surprise, found my
troubled maiden in possession of the drawing-room.   She was evidently troubled still,
and had been waiting there in the hope of
seeing me alone.   We were too quickly inter-
rupted by her parents, however, and I had
no conversation with her till I sat down to
the piano after dinner and beckoned to her
to come and stand by it.   Her father had
gone off to smoke ; her mother dozed by
one of the crackling little fires of the summer's end.

"Why didn't you come home the day you
told me you meant to ?"

She fixed her eyes on my hands.   "I
couldn't, I couldn't !"

"You look to me as if you were very ill."

"I am," the girl said, simply.

"You ought to see some one.   Something
ought to be done."

She shook her head with quiet despair.
"It would be no use — no one would
know."

"What do you mean—would know ?"

"No one would understand."

"You ought to make them !"

" Never—never !" she repeated. "Never !"

" I confess *I* don't," I replied, with a kind of angry renunciation. I played louder, with the passion of my uneasiness and the aggravation of my responsibility.

" No, you don't indeed," said Louisa Chantry.

I had only to accept this disadvantage, and after a moment I went on : " What became of Mr. Brandon ?"

" I don't know."

" Did he go away ?"

" That same evening."

" Which same evening ?"

" The day you were there. I never saw him again."

I was silent a minute, then I risked : " And you never will, eh ?"

" Never—never !"

" Then why shouldn't you get better?"

She also hesitated, after which she answered, " Because I'm going to die."

My music ceased in spite of me and we sat looking at each other. Helen Chantry woke up with a little start and asked what was the matter. I rose from the piano and I couldn't help saying, " Dear Helen, I haven't the least idea." Louisa sprang up, pressing her hand to her left side, and the next instant I cried aloud, "She's faint—she's ill—do come to her!" Mrs. Chantry bustled over to us, and immediately afterwards the girl had thrown herself on her mother's breast, as she had thrown herself days before on mine; only this time without tears, without cries, in the strangest, most tragic silence. She was not faint, she was only in despair—that at least is the way I really saw her. There was something in her contact that scared poor Helen, that operated a sudden revelation ; I can see at this hour the queer, frightened look she gave me over Louisa's shoulder. The girl, however, in a moment disengaged herself, declaring that she was not ill, only tired, very tired, and wanted to go to bed. " Take her, take her —go with her," I said to her mother ; and I pushed them, got them out of the room, partly to conceal my own trepidation. A few moments after they had gone Christopher Chantry came in, having finished

his cigar, and I had to mention to him—to
explain their absence—that his daughter
was so very fatigued that she had with-
drawn under her mother's superintendence.
" Didn't she seem done up, awfully done
up? What on earth, at that confounded
place, did she go in for?" the dear man
asked, with his pointless kindness. I
couldn't tell him this was just what I myself wanted to know; and while I pretended to read I wondered inextinguishably
what indeed she had "gone in" for. It
had become still more difficult to keep my
vow than I had expected; it was also
very difficult that evening to converse with
Christopher Chantry. His wife's continued
absence rendered some conversation necessary; yet it had the advantage of making
him remark, after it had lasted an hour,
that he must go to see what was the matter. He left me, and soon afterwards I
betook myself to my room; bedtime was
elastic in the early sense at Chantry. I
knew I should only have to wait a while for
Helen to come to me, and, in fact, by eleven
o'clock she arrived.

"She's in a very strange state—something happened there."

"And *what* happened, pray?"

"I can't make out; she won't tell me."

"Then what makes you suppose so?"

"She has broken down utterly; she says there was something."

"Then she does tell you?"

"Not a bit. She only begins, and then stops short; she says it's too dreadful."

"Too dreadful?"

"She says it's *horrible*," my poor friend murmured, with tears in her eyes and tragic speculation in her mild maternal face.

"But in what way? Does she give you no facts, no clew?"

"It was something she did."

We looked at each other a moment. "Did?" I echoed. "Did to whom?"

"She won't tell me—she says she *can't*. She tries to bring it out, but it sticks in her throat."

"Nonsense. She did nothing," I said.

"What *could* she do?" Helen asked, gazing at me.

" She's ill, she's in a fever ; her mind's wandering."

" So I say to her father."

" And what does *she* say to him ?"

"Nothing—she won't speak to him. He's with her now, but she only lies there letting him hold her hand, with her face turned away from him and her eyes closed."

" You must send for the doctor immediately."

" I've already sent for him."

" Should you like me to sit up with her ?"

"Oh, I'll do that !" Helen said. Then she asked, " But if you were there the other day, what did *you* see ?"

" Nothing whatever," I resolutely answered.

" *Really* nothing ?"

" Really, my dear child."

" But was there nobody there who could have made up to her ?"

I hesitated a moment. "My poor Helen, you should have seen them !"

" She wouldn't look at anybody that wasn't remarkably nice," Helen mused.

"Well—I don't want to abuse your friends

15

—but nobody was remarkably nice. Believe me, she hasn't looked at anybody, and nothing whatever has occurred. She's ill, and it's a mere morbid fancy."

" It's a mere morbid fancy—" Mrs. Chantry gobbled down this formula. I felt that I was giving her another still more acceptable, and which she as promptly adopted, when I added that Louisa would soon get over it.

I may as well say at once that Louisa never got over it. There followed an extraordinary week, which I look back upon as one of the most uncomfortable of my life. The doctor had something to say about the action of his patient's heart—it was weak and slightly irregular, and he was anxious to learn whether she had lately been exposed to any violent shock or emotion—but he could give no name to the disorder under the influence of which she had begun unmistakably to sink. She lay on the sofa in her room—she refused to go to bed, and in the absence of complications it was not insisted on — utterly white, weak, and abstracted, shaking her head at all suggestions, waving away all nourishment save the infinitesimally little that enabled her to stretch out her hand from time to time (at intervals of very unequal length) and begin, "Mother, mother!" as if she were mustering courage for a supreme confession. The courage never came; she was haunted by a strange impulse to speak, which in turn was checked on her lips by some deeper horror or some stranger fear. She seemed to seek relief spasmodically from some unforgetable consciousness, and then to find the greatest relief of all in impenetrable silence. I knew these things only from her mother, for before me (I went gently in and out of her room two or three times a day) she gave no sign whatever. The little local doctor, after the first day, acknowledged himself at sea, and expressed a desire to consult with a colleague at Exeter. The colleague journeyed down to us and shuffled and stammered; he recommended an appeal to a high authority in London. The high authority was summoned by telegraph and paid us a flying visit. He enunicated the valuable opinion that it was a very curious case, and dropped the striking remark that in so charming a home a young lady ought to bloom like a flower. The young lady's late hostess came over, but she could throw no light on anything; all that she had ever noticed was that Louisa had seemed "rather blue" for a day or two before she brought her visit to a close. Our days were dismal enough and our nights were dreadful, for I took turns with Helen in sitting up with the girl. Chantry Court itself seemed conscious of the riddle that made its chambers ache, it bowed its gray old head over the fate of its daughter. The people who had been coming were put off; dinner became a ceremony enacted mainly by the servants. I sat alone with Christopher Chantry, whose honest hair, in his mystification, stuck out as if he had been overhauling accounts. My hours with Louisa were even more intensely silent, for she almost never looked at me. In the watches of the night, however, I at last saw more clearly into what she was thinking of. Once when I caught her wan eyes resting upon me I took advantage of it to kneel down by her bed and speak to her with the utmost tenderness.

"If you can't say it to your mother, can you say it perhaps to *me* ?"

She gazed at me for some time. "What does it matter now—if I'm dying?"

I shook my head and smiled. "You won't die if you get it off your mind."

"You'd be cruel to him," she said. "He's innocent—he's innocent."

"Do you mean *you're* guilty? What trifle are you magnifying?"

"Do you call it a trifle—" She faltered and paused.

"Certainly I do, my dear." Then I risked a great stroke. "I've often done it myself!"

"*You ?* Never, never! I was cruel to him," she added.

This puzzled me, I couldn't work it into my conception. "How were you cruel?"

"In the garden. I changed suddenly, I drove him away, I told him he filled me with horror."

"Why did you do that?"

"Because my shame came over me."

"Your shame?"

"What I had done in the house."

"And what had you done?"

She lay a few moments with her eyes closed, as if she were living it over. "I broke out to him, I told him," she began at last. But she couldn't continue, she was powerless to utter it.

"Yes, I know what you told him. Millions of girls have told young men that before."

"They've been asked, they've been asked! They didn't speak *first!* I didn't even know him, he didn't care for me, I had seen him for the first time the day before. I said strange things to him, and he behaved like a gentleman."

"Well he might!"

"Then, before he could turn round, when we had simply walked out of the house together and strolled in the garden—it was as if I were borne along in the air by the wonder of what I had said—it rolled over me that I was lost."

" Lost ?"

" That I had been horrible — that I had been mad. Nothing could ever unsay it. I frightened him—I almost struck him."

" Poor fellow !" I smiled.

" Yes—pity him. He was kind. But he'll see me that way—always !"

I hesitated as to the answer it was best to make to this ; then I proceeded : " Don't think he'll remember you—he'll see other girls."

" Ah, he'll *forget* me !" she softly and miserably wailed ; and I saw that I had said the wrong thing. I bent over her more closely to kiss her, and when I raised my head her mother was on the other side of the bed. She fell on her knees there for the same purpose, and when Louisa felt her lips she stretched out her arms to embrace her. She had the strength to draw her close, and I heard her begin again, for the hundredth time, " Mother, mother—"

" Yes, my own darling."

Then for the hundredth time I heard her stop. There was an intensity in her silence.

It made me wildly nervous; I got up and turned away.

"Mother, mother!" the girl repeated, and poor Helen replied with a sound of passionate solicitation. But her daughter only exhaled in the waiting hush, while I stood at the window where the dawn was faint, the most miserable moan in the world. "I'm dying!" she said, articulately; and she died that night, after an hour, unconscious. The doctor arrived almost at the moment; this time he was sure it must have been the heart. The poor parents were in stupefaction, and I gave up half my visits and stayed with them a month. But in spite of their stupefaction I kept my vow.

THE END.

By BRANDER MATTHEWS.

THE STORY OF A STORY, and Other Stories.
Illustrated. 16mo, Cloth, Ornamental, $1 25.

Mr. Matthews writes as a student of life and a cultivated man of the world. He uses good English, and his stories are finished with a high degree of art. It is always a pleasure to meet with an essay in fiction from his expertly wielded pen.— *Boston Beacon.*

AMERICANISMS AND BRITICISMS, with Other Essays on Other Isms. With Portrait. 16mo, Cloth, Ornamental, $1 00.

Mr. Matthews is a clear thinker and a forcible writer, with a good solid basis of learning upon which to build his essays. We like his outright patriotism as well as his way of calling a spade by its common name. Good, wholesome, and instructive reading.—*Independent,* N. Y.

THE DECISION OF THE COURT. A Comedy. Illustrated. 32mo, Cloth, Ornamental, 50 cents.

A bright little comedietta, in which the author has shown felicity of language and a refreshing humor, which is intensified by its unpretentiousness.—*Jewish Messenger,* N. Y.

IN THE VESTIBULE LIMITED. A Story. Illustrated. 32mo, Cloth, Ornamental, 50 cents.

For compressed, swift, clear narrative, this bit of genre work in fiction is unsurpassed. As a character study it shows keen psychological insight. There is no attempt at being funny, yet the reader is continually just on the point of breaking out into laughter.—*Interior,* Chicago.

Published by HARPER & BROTHERS, N. Y.

THE ODD NUMBER SERIES.

16mo, Cloth, Ornamental.

Other volumes to follow.

Published by HARPER & BROTHERS, N. Y.

☞ *Any of the above works will be sent by mail, postage prepaid, to any part of the United States, Canada, or Mexico, on receipt of the price.*